Danger.

Lucy tried to pull free. *No more visions! Make them stop!*

But the stranger's hand squeezed tighter, sending a chaos of sensations to her very core.

Burning like the moon, red just like the moon, burning eyes, burning lips, burning souls—

"Is he?" she heard him ask again. "Is Byron *dead?*"

Lucy felt the walls sway around her, the stones shift beneath her feet. For one brief second the young man's eyes actually seemed to change color, black and amber fusing together in a liquid, luminous glow—yet she convinced herself it was only a trick of her own unshed tears. She tried to answer him—*wanted* to answer him—but her thoughts were all muddled, and she was so hot, and he was holding her so tight . . . *so tight . . .*

"Yes." *Don't make me say it—I can't bear to say it!* "Yes! He's dead!"

"You're sure?"

Memories stabbed through her head, pierced through her heart. "If you were really his brother, you wouldn't be asking me these questions! If you were really his brother, you'd already know—"

The Unseen
part 3
blood brothers

RICHIE TANKERSLEY CUSICK

speak
An Imprint of Penguin Group (USA) Inc.

SPEAK
Published by the Penguin Group
Penguin Group (USA) Inc., 345 Hudson Street, New York, New York 10014, U.S.A
Penguin Group (Canada), 90 Eglinton Avenue East, Suite 700, Toronto,
Ontario, Canada M4P 2Y3 (a division of Pearson Penguin Canada Inc.)
Penguin Books Ltd, 80 Strand, London WC2R 0RL, England
Penguin Ireland, 25 St Stephen's Green, Dublin 2, Ireland
(a division of Penguin Books Ltd)
Penguin Group (Australia), 250 Camberwell Road, Camberwell, Victoria 3124, Australia
(a division of Pearson Australia Group Pty Ltd)
Penguin Books India Pvt Ltd, 11 Community Centre, Panchsheel Park,
New Delhi - 110 017, India
Penguin Group (NZ), Cnr Airborne and Rosedale Roads, Albany, Auckland 1310,
New Zealand (a division of Pearson New Zealand Ltd)
Penguin Books (South Africa) (Pty) Ltd, 24 Sturdee Avenue, Rosebank,
Johannesburg 2196, South Africa

Registered Offices: Penguin Books Ltd, 80 Strand, London WC2R 0RL, England

First published in the UK by Scholastic Ltd, 2005
Published by Speak, an imprint of Penguin Group (USA) Inc., 2006

1 3 5 7 9 10 8 6 4 2

Copyright © Richie Tankersley Cusick, 2005
All rights reserved

LIBRARY OF CONGRESS CATALOGING-IN-PUBLICATION DATA
Cusick, Richie Tankersley.
Blood brothers / by Richie Tankersley Cusick.
p.   cm. — (The unseen ; pt. 3)
Summary: A stranger claiming to be Byron's brother appears, horribly wounded, and
throws Lucy's life into further turmoil.
ISBN 0-14-240583-3 (pbk.)
[1. Supernatural—Fiction. 2. Mistaken identity—Fiction.] I. Title.
PZ7.C9646Blo 2006 [Fic]—dc22 2005051630

Printed in the United States of America

To Anne with love—for saving
me so many times
in so many different ways . . .

Thank you, my friend
You will always be my better half.

Prologue

He'd had to think quickly.

After this last kill he'd been so gorged, so utterly exhausted from frenzy and frustration, he'd been unable to return to his bed. He'd been forced to seek out another hiding place . . . and then he'd crept inside and he'd slept.

Slept far past his normal hour of waking . . .

Slept right through the day . . . into the night . . .

Slept the fathomless sleep of the dead.

He'd never seen the attack coming.

Never awakened fully, even, until the first hot spurt of blood, the first scream of ripping flesh, the whole world exploding in a thick, wet fountain of scarlet and black.

He had no idea which of them had struck the first blow. Or when instinct had taken ahold of him, every primal sense honed for survival, no matter what the pain, no matter what the cost . . .

He did not remember which had been the last to fall . . .

He was only and finally aware of the silence and the peace. The wind upon his face, the snow upon his lips. He was thirsty, yet could not seem to drink. He needed warmth and shelter, yet could not seem to move.

He was in desperate agony, yet could not help himself.

And so he lay there, stunned and weakened, too sick to lick his wounds. Until at last, and like a dream, the sound of quiet footsteps had floated through his mind . . .

He heard them from a distance, moving closer and closer, phantom footsteps of no real concern, no imminent danger. But as he struggled to comprehend them, he realized these footsteps were no dream at all.

They were real, and they were human.

They were coming toward the burial place, dangerously close to where he rested.

And so he'd had to think quickly.

Think quickly and act with haste.

Transform to a shadow? Mist? A guise of the living, a memory of the dead?

Or, in one swift, smooth motion, ready himself to strike again?

But then he paused, consumed by an ache so deep he had not even realized he moaned.

For now he saw this was no enemy.

Now he realized this was Lucy—*his Lucy*—approaching him unaware and unsuspecting, steeped in grief and sorrow as he had always known her.

And yet . . . different somehow.

Unsettlingly different, somehow.

He could feel it, as sharply as he could feel the rats cowering around him, their ears twitching in fear, their glowing eyes averted from his own, their teeth stained red from the remnants of his meal and the raw meat of his wound. And he could smell it, too—as surely as he smelled the slow and steady creeping of decay, the lingering despair of so many wasted lives rotting in the graves around him.

No, Lucy was not quite the same as before.

3

Something had changed since he'd last laid eyes upon her.

Despite her confusion, there was now resolve.

And amid her fear and helplessness burned a new strength—small yet, to be sure, but solid with determination.

How interesting, he thought . . . *and how curious.*

And also how very delightful.

So delightful, it made him smile, despite his anguish.

He couldn't help wondering what had happened—*one incident? or many?*—to touch her at such a profound level in so short a time.

But no matter.

This newfound strength of Lucy's would only serve to make the Game more interesting. More challenging. More worth winning.

So he'd narrowed his eyes and waited.

Waited until her footsteps were practically upon him.

Until, in one more second, Lucy would be at the gates of the mausoleum, peering into the shadows of the tomb, stepping across that crumbling threshold between life and death.

Could he take her? As this desperate need for her surged through every vein, filling him with brief and savage power?

Yes . . . yes! Take her now!

But he did not.

He thought quickly instead.

And felt that explosive rush of skin and muscles shifting, features rearranging, as quick as a heartbeat, as natural as breath.

So now he could listen.

Stay close and watch.

And like so many times before, Lucy would never even know.

1

She hadn't expected the cemetery to look so spooky at this hour of the morning.

Like wandering phantoms, tatters of soft white mist hovered among the graves, and an unnatural quiet smothered the sound of Lucy's footsteps as she made her way to the remote section of the burial grounds. The dead slept deep and undisturbed. Remembered and forgotten alike, they surrounded her on all sides, rotting peacefully to dust.

In the distance, the Wetherly mausoleum came darkly into view, silhouetted against the gloom. As Lucy got nearer, she could see the wrought-iron gates and stone angels that guarded it, and for one unsettling moment, she remembered her dream about Byron and his warning.

"Keep away . . . there's no one in this place."

An icy shudder worked its way up her spine. Hesitating, she dug her hands into her coat pockets and glanced back over her shoulder.

Come on, Lucy, get a grip.

It was easy to imagine eerie whispers and invisible watchers in a creepy place like this— what had she been thinking anyway, coming here so early?

Stop scaring yourself. Nobody here can hurt you.

Giving herself a stern mental shake, she walked over to the front of the tomb. To her surprise, the double gates weren't padlocked as she'd assumed they'd be—in fact, they were standing partway open, one of them creaking rustily as the breeze swung it back and forth.

Heart quickening, Lucy glanced around a second time.

If someone *were* here, they'd be impossible to see, she admitted to herself. Anyone could be hiding close by or far away.

Lucy suppressed another shiver.

Turning in a slow circle, she scanned the graves and headstones, the sepulchres and statues, the trees and shadows and mist. A taste

7

of fear crept into her throat, and she tried to choke it down.

Cautiously, she turned back to the gates.

Taking one in each hand, she eased them open the rest of the way. Cracks had widened along the foundation, and leaves had sifted in over the broken, weathered stones of the floor.

Holding her breath, Lucy walked into the crypt.

She saw the muddy footprints and tufts of clotted hair, the dark, reddish-brown stains smeared along the walls . . .

But she didn't see the figure behind her.

Not till she turned and screamed and stumbled from his arms, trying wildly to fight her way free.

And then she stared up, shocked, into eyes as black and deep as midnight.

"Oh my God," she choked. "Who are you?"

The dark-haired young man gazed coolly back at her.

"Byron's brother," he answered. "Who the hell are *you*?"

2

He could almost have *been* Byron.

The likeness was so incredible that for one wild moment Lucy actually glanced around at the walls of the mausoleum, as though Byron himself might have stepped from his burial place to stand before her now.

And yet, in one swift moment of scrutiny, she could see that there were differences. Differences not only obvious, but subtle as well—differences she felt certain of but couldn't totally define. Even in that moment of shock, Lucy sensed a sadness even more complicated than Byron's, and a raw sensitivity far beyond any that Byron had ever shown.

She wanted to look away but was transfixed. At first glance, she'd mistaken his eyes for that same midnight black that Byron's had been, but now that she was closer, she could see they were actually a deep amber color, surrounding unusually large black pupils. The effect of this was a wide, unwavering stare that Lucy found both disturbing and fascinating, and as he held her gaze, she noted that his eyes never blinked.

Lucy guessed him to be about the same height and weight as Byron, with the same lean build. His face was less rugged, his cheekbones every bit as prominent, his nose more slender, his features slightly more delicate. He had a high forehead and low curved brows, the same faint beard shadow along his jaws and chin and upper lip. His perfectly shaped mouth looked both sensuous and seductive; his dark straight hair, parting naturally in the middle, fell to just below his ears.

Weary shadows rimmed his eyes. Shadows like bruises, hollowing his cheeks and accentuating the unnatural ghost-white pallor of his skin. And slashing downward from his left ear to the right side of his chin was a long, jagged scar that seemed very deep and very old.

In this quick instant of observation, two bizarre thoughts flashed unexpectedly into Lucy's mind.

That he was perhaps the most beautiful young man she'd ever seen in her entire life.

And that he and Byron could have been magically superimposed, like two photographs layered together, forming a familiar, yet brand-new face.

"Byron . . ."

Without even realizing it, she whispered the name. And though the stranger's gaze had seemed to stop time, Lucy jolted back to awareness, realizing that only seconds had passed.

Realizing he *wasn't* Byron.

This stranger, this bold trespasser standing before her now, *wasn't* Byron, could *never* be Byron. Byron was dead, Byron was out of her life forever, Byron had no brother or she would have *known*; he would have *told* her. It was all too much—too much to absorb, too much to process—and suddenly Lucy realized that she was having trouble breathing, that her throat was closing up.

"Who are you?" she heard the young man ask again, but his voice was like a dream, and Lucy couldn't answer.

She felt as if she was suffocating. The air in

the mausoleum was thick and heavy, settling over her like folds of velvet, crushing her with a sweetness that was almost sickening.

She knew that sweetness.

She'd smelled it before, that cloying fragrance of allure and elusion, but where was it coming from now? It hadn't been in the mausoleum when she'd gotten here—*had it?* Could she have somehow not realized?

Turning, she looked down at the dark red stains upon the stones, the clotted hair along the floor. Her mind reeled backward, back to the cave and back to her terror. *Dark splatters over the ground . . . dark smears trailing back into the tunnel where light couldn't reach . . .*

No, it's not the same, she tried to convince herself. *This grisly scene has nothing to do with the other: this was just some stray animal, this can be explained.*

But she was starting to feel light-headed and confused. Was this the scent of blood? The aftermath of fear? The lingering odor of death?

"What do you want?"

Had the stranger spoken aloud just now? Had *she?*

Lucy put her hands to her temples and tried

to concentrate. Bring herself back into focus. He was still staring at her, as though he didn't even notice the sweet, sultry odor enclosing them. What was wrong with him? Surely he could smell it—how could he not smell it?

Yet even as she started to mention it to him, the sweetness was already fading. And then a cold, raw breeze snaked through the tomb, and the fragrance vanished completely.

But the young man hadn't gone. The young man hadn't disappeared with the blast of the wind; he was still here, gazing down at her with a frown more curious than threatening.

Brother . . .

The word whispered softly through her head. Once again she wondered if one of them had spoken, or if the thought had simply crept unbidden into her subconscious.

"You didn't know?" His lips were moving now. His voice was deep like Byron's . . . soft like Byron's . . .

Brother . . . of course . . . that would explain the resemblance . . .

"You're not Byron's brother," Lucy said.

Her voice was strong with resolve, with a

13

defiance that surprised her. And then came the anger, fierce and possessive, rushing through her like fire. How dare this stranger encroach into Byron's resting place—how dare he claim Byron's name! Her insides were trembling, grief transformed to protective rage, as though she were facing down something evil that had crept onto hallowed ground.

She lifted her chin, fists clenched tightly at her sides. "Byron doesn't *have* a brother."

"Is that what he told you?" the young man countered. He sounded exhausted, too empty for any sort of emotion.

"Yes, he—"

Lucy stopped, suddenly unsure. What *had* Byron told her? He'd talked about Katherine and his grandmother, about himself when he was a child.

He'd never said anything about having a brother.

But then again, he'd never actually said that he didn't.

Flustered, Lucy gazed back at the stranger. He was leaning a little toward one wall, his left arm pressed close to his side. *He must be freezing*, she

14

thought, and no wonder, dressed as he was in ragged jeans and T-shirt, scruffy denim jacket and dirty old boots. He'd looked pale before, but now he was even whiter. His skin seemed paperlike, almost translucent, and for the first time she noticed the slight trembling of his hands.

"I don't believe you." *Even though you look so much like Byron, even though you sound so much like Byron, even though I wish you were Byron because you've made my heart ache all over again.* "Matt would have told me if he'd found you."

"I don't know who you're talking about." He hesitated briefly. "And nobody knows I'm here."

"Then you'd better leave before I call the police."

"That wouldn't be a very smart thing to do."

Backing away, Lucy drew herself to full height. "Are you threatening me?"

"No, I'm just saying—" He broke off, breath catching sharply in his throat, and Lucy watched as he braced himself against the wall and clamped his arm tighter to his side.

"I'm just saying," he continued softly, "that I'm not particularly fond of authority figures, and I wish you wouldn't call them."

Lucy kept her eyes on him. "Why not? Are you in some kind of trouble?"

"That would be a very long story."

"Go ahead. I've got time."

"Not *that* much time, I'm afraid." One corner of his mouth twisted, though whether from bitterness or amusement, it was hard to tell. "You were close to Byron?"

The question caught Lucy off guard. As she fumbled for an answer, she saw those strange amber eyes of his glide smoothly down her body, then up again to her face, with an almost suggestive—and calculated—slowness.

"Close?" Cheeks flushing, Lucy did her best to recover. "I was . . . am . . . a friend."

"You must have known him well."

Again Lucy hesitated. "I didn't know him very long. Only a few days."

"That's more than just friendship I see in your eyes."

Startled, she glanced away. She remembered the secret Byron had shared with her—his ability to view people's souls through their eyes. Was this stranger referring to something that only Byron's brother could have known? Lucy forced herself to look back at him, but his expression revealed nothing.

"You don't know anything about me," she said angrily.

"You might be surprised."

It was a quiet answer, and matter-of-fact, but one that sent a chill through Lucy's heart. It was all she could do to keep her voice level. "What's that supposed to mean?"

His right hand lifted to fend off her question. With growing dismay, Lucy watched a violent shudder work through him, gnawing deep into his muscles. He bent lower, lips tightening, skin like chalk. His eyes squeezed shut, then opened again, seeking her out as though she'd suddenly gone invisible.

"Is Byron really dead?" he murmured.

He was still shivering but trying not to show it, easing himself onto his knees, left arm still clutched to his side. For a panicked moment she wondered if he might be on drugs or out of his mind—maybe even dying. Whatever was wrong with him, he was definitely in no shape to chase her, she decided. Now was her chance to run away, drive off, call for help. He even seemed a little disoriented; with any luck, he might not even notice she'd gone.

But he was between her and the doorway, and Lucy had to get past him. And even though there was enough space to slip by, something held her back. Something about the way he just knelt there, shoulders slumped, head bowed, his dark profile in sharp relief against the white marble of the crypt, seeming so alone . . .

She made a run for it.

With lightning speed he caught her, right arm flinging out, fingers clamping tight around her wrist.

Lucy gasped at the shock. Not just the iciness of his skin or the alarming strength of his grip, but the images that exploded through her brain.

Sweet night—leaves, stars, moonlight patterns— shadows swift on silent feet—dark desires deep as open wounds—wind flowing like blood, streaming like blood, hot wild fountains and rivers of blood— screams from secret places, screams that no one hears, pleasure pain and begging screams of terror and surrender . . .

No! Lucy tried to pull free. *No more visions! Make them stop!*

But the stranger's hand squeezed tighter, sending a chaos of sensations to her very core.

Burning . . .

"Please—"

Burning lungs, burning skin, burning eyes . . .

"Let go!"

Burning like the moon, red just like the moon, burning eyes, burning lips, burning souls—

"Is he?" she heard him ask again. "Is Byron *dead?*"

Lucy felt the walls sway around her, the stones shift beneath her feet. For one brief second the young man's eyes actually seemed to change color, black and amber fusing together in a liquid, luminous glow—yet she convinced herself it was only a trick of her own unshed tears. She tried to answer him—*wanted* to answer him—but her thoughts were all muddled, and she was so hot, and he was holding her so tight . . . *so tight . . .*

"Yes." *Don't make me say it—I can't bear to say it!* "Yes! He's dead!"

"You're sure?"

Memories stabbed through her head, pierced through her heart. "If you were really his

19

brother, you wouldn't be asking me these questions! If you were really his brother, you'd already know—"

"How . . . long?"

He could barely gasp out the words. There was sweat along his brow and upper lip, though his breath hung like frost in the air. Lucy felt sick with both sympathy and dread.

"What is it?" she begged him. "What's wrong?"

"How long ago?"

Her mind raced feverishly, trying to find the answer. How long *had* it been since Byron died? Already much too long. Forever. A heart-breaking eternity.

"Days?" Strength was draining from his fingers; he fumbled for a tighter grasp. *"Weeks?"*

"Weeks. A couple of weeks—"

"Was there a funeral?"

"Yes."

"A service? A special service?"

"Some kind of service, yes—"

"A casket?"

As hard as she tried to prevent them, more unwanted memories flooded in. The gloomy day, the weeping crowd of mourners. The priest in black, the flowers and personal keepsakes arranged upon the coffin. She couldn't hold back tears any longer. They ran down her cheeks and dripped on the hand that held her.

"And there's no mistake?" he persisted. "There couldn't possibly be some mistake? You're absolutely sure he's dead?"

"I . . . " Sobs rose into her throat, though she stubbornly fought them down. "I was with him when he died."

His fingers slid from her arm. As Lucy stepped away and began rubbing circulation back into her wrist, she heard the hollow sound of his whisper.

"So . . . it's true, then."

Free to escape now, Lucy realized she couldn't. Something about the tonelessness of his voice, the defeated sag of his shoulders, held her there in a conflict of emotions. She watched in silence as he eased himself back against the wall, legs splayed in front of him, head bent to his chest. His right hand lifted in slow motion, fingers gliding back through his tangled mane of hair.

"Byron." Had he choked just then? Laughed? Sobbed? His voice was so faint, Lucy could barely hear. "Damn you, Byron . . ."

Her heart caught at the words. She didn't know what to do. What to say. What to think or even believe. Something inside her felt the need to comfort him; something inside her still sensed a threat. Finally, in spite of herself, she took a cautious step toward him and reached out for his shoulder.

"After all this time," he murmured.

Lucy stopped, hand poised in midair. "What?" she asked him gently.

He lifted his head and rested it back against the wall. He wasn't looking at her anymore. In truth, he didn't even seem to realize she was there.

"After all this time," he murmured again. "And now I'm too late."

3

Lucy was at a complete loss. One minute ago she'd been ready to turn him in; now she felt as if *she* were the intruder.

This can't be happening.

She glanced longingly toward the door of the mausoleum, judging her distance and her odds. The young man's eyes had closed; his body was very still. He didn't seem nearly as dangerous as he had before, only empty and sad and tired.

Stop feeling sorry for him—you don't know anything about this guy! You don't know what he's talking about, if he's even telling the truth. Haven't you gotten yourself in enough trouble already? Get out of here—now!—while you have the chance!

"I wouldn't, if I were you," he warned her.

Lucy froze. How had he known what she was thinking? His eyes were still shut, his face

23

turned from her own. Once more an uneasy feeling grabbed hold of her, as though not only her body were vulnerable to him, but her thoughts as well.

"You're not very good at being quiet." The effort of conversation seemed to be becoming too much for him. "And I doubt you'd get very far."

He opened his eyes and tried to focus on her feet. As Lucy followed his gaze, she realized that she'd actually inched closer to the doorway, without even being aware. But obviously *he* had been aware—even without watching.

Simple explanation, Lucy. He can't read minds— he just has very good ears.

"So what are you saying?" Feeling braver, she took several more steps toward freedom. It was obvious he couldn't even stand now, much less pursue her. "Why wouldn't I get far? Are you going to stop me?"

"No. But something out there will."

Lucy stared at him. She could see that his eyes had shifted yet again, peering out through the shadows and tentacles of fog, far beyond the open gates of the mausoleum. Terror clutched at her heart. And when she finally spoke, her voice shook with anger as well as with fear.

"I'm going. I don't know who you are, but you're not Byron's brother. And I'm calling the police, whether you like it or not."

She made it as far as the door when she saw it—the slow, subtle movement beneath a nearby overhang of trees. It seemed to slink among the graves, a long lean silhouette, low to the ground, then silently disappeared behind a headstone. Lucy felt the hairs prickle at the back of her neck. She'd had that feeling earlier of being followed, and she'd managed to convince herself that it was only her imagination. But now . . .

"It's only a shadow," she said firmly. "There's nothing out there but shadows."

Yet glancing back, she saw the young man struggling up from the floor. His face contorted in pain, and with a feeble gesture that was almost protective, he motioned her to come closer.

Lucy stayed where she was. In a rush of indecision, she wondered which would be worse—to take her chances in here or in the cemetery. She couldn't see anything moving out

25

there now . . . whatever she thought she'd seen was gone. If, in fact, it had ever really been there to begin with.

There was no time to make up her mind. She heard a groan behind her—scarcely louder than a sigh—and as she turned around, the stranger sank to his knees and collapsed. Only this time, as Lucy's eyes swept over him, she noticed the trail of dark liquid spreading out from his side, pooling across the floor.

"Oh my God."

She was beside him in an instant. She whispered to him, but sensed that he was far beyond answering. With growing horror she gazed down at the large wet stain on his jacket, then carefully lifted it away. His T-shirt was soaked, plastered to his side. His body and clothes reeked of blood. Taking a deep breath, Lucy began peeling the T-shirt from his skin, bracing herself for whatever she might find.

But nothing could have prepared her. Not even in her worst nightmares.

With a shocked cry, Lucy whirled away. Bile rose into the back of her throat, and she covered her mouth with trembling hands. And though his critical condition was instantly clear to her, it still seemed an eternity before she was able to compose herself and turn back to the gruesome sight.

At first she thought he'd been stabbed.

But then, as the true horror of it sank in, she realized that something had bitten him.

Bitten savagely into his side, leaving sharp, jagged teeth marks around a gaping hole of raw flesh and stringy muscle, gnawed bones, and dangling shreds of skin.

Dead leaves were mashed into the wound. Leaves and grass and dirt all mixed together into a bloody paste, as though some primal instinct had guided him in a desperate attempt at survival.

How he'd managed to survive even this long was past her understanding.

Lucy couldn't stop shaking. As she tilted her head back and drew in an enormous gulp of air, she willed herself not to throw up. What could have happened to him? What sort of creature could have done this? With an instinctive reflex of her own, she pulled off her wool scarf and coat and the sweater beneath it. Her undershirt was light, but she scarcely felt the cold. In fact, she didn't feel much of anything now except a strange sense of unreality.

She wadded her sweater into a ball. She lowered it to his side, then hesitated a moment, steeling her nerves. From some deep level of anguish he moaned again, as though subconsciously aware of what would come next. And as she pressed the sweater carefully against his wound, she felt a warm flow of blood, slick on her fingers.

"I'm sorry." Despite her resolve, Lucy's voice quivered. "I don't mean to hurt you . . . but you've got to stay very still."

She didn't expect him to answer. But when he did, his words chilled her.

"Nothing . . . nothing you can do . . ."

Lucy's heart sank. Was he telling her it was hopeless? Could he feel his life slipping away, even as she fought to save it?

"Shh . . . don't talk." As gently as she could, she worked the scarf under him and around him, using it as a makeshift tourniquet, tying the sweater firmly in place. Then she covered him with her coat and tried to think what to do.

Whoever this young man was, she didn't want to leave him. She couldn't bear the thought of his lying here cold and suffering and all alone, maybe even dying before she could get back. Yet there was no way she could manage him by herself. And even if she could, just moving him would probably do more harm than good.

Lucy made up her mind. "I'm going for help. I'll be back as quick as I can."

Had he heard her? He was lying so still, his eyes closed, and he didn't appear to be breathing. Terrified, she pressed her fingers to the side of his neck and searched for a pulse.

She jumped as his hand brushed hers. There were no visions this time—only a brief sense of fading light, like a candle burning low, or the moon slipping behind a cloud. The feeling was gone in an instant, and she wondered why she hadn't seen him move, why she hadn't felt even the slightest shifting of his body.

"Not . . . safe here . . ." he murmured. His eyes were still shut, and, to Lucy's horror, a trickle of blood oozed from one corner of his mouth. Bending closer, she smoothed the damp hair from his forehead and willed herself to stay calm.

"That's why you need a doctor. I've got a phone in my car, and I'll come right back, I promise. And then we can get you to the hospital—"

"No . . . please . . ." Even in his whisper, Lucy heard desperation. He tried to lift his head, but couldn't. His face was drenched with sweat, and the scar slicing his left cheek was like a jagged crack through ice.

"Listen to me," she said firmly. "You've *got* to go to the emergency room." Didn't he realize what was happening? Didn't he realize how seriously he was hurt? "I think you're going into shock—you're bleeding really badly—"

"No . . . no hospital."

"Don't you understand what I'm telling you? You could *die!*"

"Not . . . dying. Not . . . what it seems . . ."

He was rambling now, she was sure of it—out of his head with pain, making no sense whatsoever. But as she started to get up, his desperate whisper stopped her once again.

"Don't . . . leave me here. Please . . . *please*. I'm begging you. For Byron's sake."

All the argument went out of her. In stunned

30

silence she gazed down at his face, a face that could have been Byron's own death mask, a face growing blurry now beyond her quick swell of tears. Then at last she sat back on her heels, surrendering with a reluctant nod.

"What do you want me to do?"

His lips barely parted. "Somewhere . . . safe."

"But that's what I'm trying to tell you—I *am* trying to take you somewhere safe—"

"Close . . ."

"There's *nothing* close!" Frustrated, Lucy stood up and gestured futilely toward the gates of the mausoleum. "There's only *here*—and—and the *cemetery*! And my *car*! And—and—that old *church* over there!"

"Church?"

Perhaps it was only a trick of the shadows, but for a second she could almost have sworn that his eyes opened, fixing her with a wide, dark stare. And though he'd barely managed to utter that one word, it seemed to hang in the air between them now, like some strange and ominous echo.

"Church," he murmured again. "Yes . . . take me there . . ."

31

But she *must* have imagined that unnerving stare of his, because he was still sprawled there like a lifeless doll, and his head was turned away; he wasn't even looking at her.

"It's only used for storage now," she tried to explain. "I don't even know if we can get in."

He didn't answer. Suddenly fearing the worst, Lucy dropped down beside him again, her voice urgent.

"Please! Don't give up! You've got to hang on! *Stay* with me!"

Despite his wounds, she shook him violently. The smell of blood was stronger now, rusty at the back of her throat. She realized it was all over her—on her jeans and shoes and shirt, her hands, even strands of her hair. She wiped her palms across her thighs, but the red stains wouldn't come off. Terrified, she shook him again and was relieved to see a flicker of movement behind his eyelids.

Oh God . . . what am I going to do?

His breath was so shallow; she could hear a faint gurgling in his lungs. She pressed one hand to his chest, just to make sure his heart was still beating. Feeling more frantic by the second, she tucked her coat snugly around him, then got up and hurried to the door.

Soft gray light was spreading through the mausoleum. Outside the fog was beginning to lift. Yet despite the urgency of the situation, Lucy hesitated and peered off through the crooked headstones and fading shadows of the cemetery.

He said something was out there. He said it wasn't safe.

Lucy choked down a taste of fear. She wrapped her arms around herself and shivered violently.

Something real? Something stalking? Watching? Slinking between those graves?

"It's gone now," he whispered, and Lucy spun around, startled.

She was absolutely certain this time that he hadn't moved. Hadn't turned his body even a fraction of an inch, hadn't lifted up his head. He couldn't possibly have seen her watching the graveyard, couldn't possibly have heard her silent thoughts.

Which made it even more frightening when he whispered to her again.

"Hurry . . . before it comes back."

4

Déjà vu . . .

As Lucy ran through the cemetery, a bad-dream feeling ran with her, clawing with icy fingers, tearing at her mind.

A twisted reality all too familiar.

A trapped-in-a-nightmare feeling that had become her life.

Déjà vu over and over and over again . . .

Neither thoughts nor things made sense anymore.

There was only madness and evil. Darkness and danger.

And a hell she would never escape.

These were the ideas that mocked her as she ran—swift, sharp flashes of panic and hope-lessness that numbed her long before she reached the old church. Her lungs burned with cold, but she swallowed the pain. She couldn't feel her legs, but her body kept going. She stumbled over neglected graves that pressed close to the side of the building; she wove through a maze of nameless headstones crowded together at the back. And as she finally reached the entrance, she couldn't help but glance in every direction, just to make sure she was alone.

"Hurry . . . before it comes back . . ."

How had he known, she wondered—how had the stranger known about that invisible presence back there in the shadows? That presence lurking so near, on the other side of the fog? And the way he'd spoken about it . . . warned her about it . . . almost as though it were something . . .

Familiar.

The word whispered through her head, and Lucy shuddered. Scrambling for a foothold on the icy stoop, she grabbed the door handle and pulled.

The church was locked.

She wrestled with the latch, but it held solid; she could hear no sounds at all from inside. Once more she glanced toward the sidewalk and the dead-end street beyond. *This is insane! That person you left back there is going to die! His life is in your hands, and you've let him talk you into something completely stupid! He needs to be in a hospital! You're wasting precious time!*

Furiously chiding herself, Lucy took off around the corner of the building. There had to be another way in—a back door, a window, something!

He's going to die, and it's your fault!

Broken stained-glass windows loomed high above her head. There were gaping holes in the eaves, and patches of rotted wood on the roof, but they were impossible to reach.

How would she ever get him here? There was no way she could carry him; she couldn't just drag him through the cemetery. *Like I dragged that headstone through the hall and onto the porch, that headstone with Angela's name on it . . .*

Her panic grew worse; her thoughts grew jumbled. What was she going to do about that headstone, anyway? She had to get home, make sure it was still hidden. What if Irene went out to get the morning paper and discovered the headstone instead?

Why are you thinking about that now? Why are you thinking about that while someone's dying?

Not someone. Byron's brother.

"No!" Lucy whispered angrily to herself. "He's not Byron's brother; Byron would have told me!"

Then why are you helping him? Why aren't you taking him to a doctor—why are you doing what he asked you to do?

"I don't know!"

She couldn't answer that—didn't *want* to answer that. She had to find shelter, but there were no doors along here, no way to get in, no place to be safe. *"Hurry,"* he'd said, *"hurry before it comes back."* Just a few months ago she'd have thought he was crazy; she'd have left him there and called the police, and her conscience would have been perfectly clear. Just a few months ago she wouldn't have listened, she wouldn't have believed him at all . . .

But that was months ago.

And that was before.

Before her world had turned upside down.

"Hurry . . . before it comes back . . ."

He'd known something was out there in the

cemetery, watching from the shadows, slipping through the fog.

And she'd known it, too.

In fact, she realized now that she'd known it all along, ever since that first cold chill of danger near Byron's grave. That sinister presence haunting her, as merciless as any recurring nightmare . . . that nameless specter she'd be forced to recognize one day . . .

Soon, Lucy.

She remembered the message in her notebook, the message that had so mysteriously disappeared—disappeared without the slightest trace, just like that phantom among the headstones . . .

Soon.

Lucy was half frozen. She sloshed through a mire of slush and snow, waded through dead, tangled shrubbery. Wind pierced the thin fabric of her shirt and gnawed her bare hands. And no matter how hard she tried to concentrate, her mind kept filling with thoughts she didn't want to think about and memories she wanted to forget.

Wanda Carver's death hung over her like a

pall—the visions she'd had of it weighed her down with guilt. She'd come here alone this morning for no other purpose than being close to Byron. She longed to feel the companionship of his spirit, a haven of peace and solitude where she wouldn't be blamed or judged. A refuge where she could sort out her thoughts, where she might understand what was happening and why.

And now this.

This mysterious stranger, bleeding to death in the Wetherly mausoleum. This stranger who claimed to be Byron's brother. She didn't even know his name.

First Katherine . . . then Byron . . .

Each encounter had led Lucy straight into tragedy and heartbreak.

Where would *this* one take her?

"Damnit!"

The ground was more slippery behind the church, and Lucy was forced to slow down. She noticed a door at the top of some steps, but it was boarded over with thick wooden beams. Frustrated, she turned and looked back at the cemetery. She'd felt so strong when she'd gotten here this morning, so capable and determined—and now, though that resolve hadn't entirely disappeared, it *had* taken a dramatic and unexpected shift. *Why are you so shocked?* Hadn't she told herself this was all she could ever expect from now on? An isolated world that became more surreal with every day? Bad surprises at every turn?

Lucy stared miserably at the old building. Where else could she go? She should never have come here in the first place—it might already be too late. As if there weren't enough deaths on her conscience already . . .

And then she spotted the cellar.

At least, she guessed it was a cellar. One of those old-fashioned ones, with double doors slanted up from the ground and opening from the middle. The door handles were looped together with a heavy chain, but there didn't appear to be a padlock. Lucy squatted down and began tugging. Apparently no one had used this entrance for a long time—the chain was heavily caked with dirt and rust, some of the links embedded into the rotting wood of the doors. After several minutes of intense struggling, she finally felt it give way, and it rattled to the ground.

Lucy hesitated, an ironic thought flitting through her mind. This was breaking and entering, wasn't it? Even though she didn't intend to take anything, wasn't she still breaking the law?

Yet trespassing into a church was far better than letting someone die, she told herself. And with that bitter reality hanging over her, she went to work on the doors.

They opened fairly easily. As a wave of dank air washed over her, Lucy peered down into a pitch-black hole, then steadied herself against the outer wall. The darkness . . . the musty smell . . . it was almost like being back in that cave again, and it took her several seconds to catch her breath. *Go on!* Yet she couldn't make herself move, and the pale morning light seemed to hesitate at the very threshold of those cellar doors. *Like an entrance to the underworld,* Lucy thought, then wondered why she had. It might be run-down, but it was still a church. *What a weird comparison to make.*

Very carefully, she inched forward. To her

relief there was a rickety flight of stairs, and as her eyes began adjusting to the gloom, more of the interior came into hazy focus. It wasn't as cold down here as she'd expected. Fresh air was already blowing in behind her, thinning out the stale, stagnant odor of neglect. She continued slowly to the bottom of the steps, wishing she had a flashlight. Silence lay thick around her, as thick as the spiderwebs crusting the walls and rafters. No footprints had disturbed the dust upon the concrete floor. Whatever parts of the cellar were being used for storage, it was obvious this tiny, cramped room hadn't been touched in quite a while.

Yet through the dim shadows, Lucy could definitely see clutter. Stacks of folding chairs and tables, cardboard boxes and wooden crates of every shape and size, a broken lectern, everything shrouded in layers and layers of dust. Stained-glass cutouts were piled on a desk; panes of glass were angled into a corner. Mysterious shapes lurked under drop cloths. An open carton held a jumble of crosses and crucifixes, while another was stuffed with candles. There were old clothes jammed into grocery bags.

From crooked picture frames along one wall saints gazed down at her, martyrs beheld her with wide and glassy stares, while Jesus himself in various poses seemed to follow her movements with a sad, forgiving smile.

In a matter of seconds, Lucy had scanned the entire area, her gaze finally coming to rest on a door in the opposite wall. It was hardly noticeable, camouflaged as it was between floor-to-ceiling shelves, and when she tried the knob, she found it locked from the other side. Backing away, she took one last inventory of the shelves and their contents—urns and incense burners, candlesticks, smashed bows and ribbons, vases, dirty altar cloths, and plastic flowers tangled into pathetic bouquets.

Definitely not the Hilton, she thought.

But a perfect room for hiding.

Warmer and drier than outside, at least. And out of the way, where nobody ever came.

And it wasn't exactly as if she was doing anything wrong, she told herself.

After all, the stranger was wounded and helpless.

What possible harm could he be?

5

He was lying just as she'd left him, sprawled there on the cold floor of the mausoleum.

Blood had thickened around his clothes and congealed beneath his arms.

When Lucy couldn't see him breathing, she thought he was dead.

It seemed an eternity that she stood there, paralyzed with fear, praying to be wrong, begging for a miracle. He looked *so much* like Byron—how could he possibly *not* be related? Just seeing him like this, suffering like this, ripped Lucy's heart in two. *You can't die! It's like losing Byron all over again!*

And suddenly, more than ever, it didn't matter to her what the truth turned out to be—who this stranger really was, or why he'd shown up here out of nowhere on this particular morning.

All that mattered to her now was that he *lived*.

She hadn't been able to save Katherine. She hadn't been able to save Byron. But she *would* save this stranger. This brother of Byron's, this nearly identical twin of Byron's—she would *not* allow him to die.

She gently placed her hand upon his back. There was an almost imperceptible rising and falling of his shoulders, and she breathed a sigh of relief.

"It's all right—it's me," she told him. "And I've found a place to take you. I just don't know how I'm going to get you there."

Had he understood her? Lucy couldn't be sure, so she gently stroked his forehead, smoothed his hair from his eyes. He was burning hot with fever. His hands were ice cold. Was his body still fighting, she wondered—or was it giving up?

"Please." She tried one more time. "Please let me bring someone. Please let me call a doctor—"

"Won't . . . help."

"Don't say that. Don't even think it."

"Can't . . . do anything . . ."

"Yes, he *could* do something for you, if you'd *let* him!"

"Already . . . already healing . . ."

Healing! Frustrated, Lucy pressed her hands to her temples and shook her head. "No, you're *not* healing! Don't you understand, you're very, very sick!"

But of course it wouldn't do any good to argue with him—he was still incoherent with shock; he didn't even know what he was saying.

"Let me . . . lean on you," he whispered, and once again Lucy placed a calming hand on his forehead.

"We can try. But it's dangerous for you to move."

"More . . . dangerous . . . here."

In spite of herself, Lucy glanced back over her shoulder, out through the gates of the mausoleum, out to the cemetery beyond. The fog had practically vanished, leaving cold, gray light in its wake. Snow clouds hung low over the trees. She could see the black silhouette of the old church looming against a sunless sky.

"If you won't let me call a doctor, then at

least let me call a friend," Lucy urged. "Some-one we can trust, who won't tell anyone—"

"Help me up."

Later she would wonder how the two of them ever made it to the cellar.

How she'd slipped her arms beneath him, oh so gently . . . coaxing him onto his good side . . . easing him up so that his head rested on her shoulder. Feeling his heart beat so faintly against her. Feeling the shallow whisper of his breath against her cheek.

She'd tied the sleeves of her coat around his neck to keep him warm. And she'd told him not to be afraid.

She didn't recall pulling him to his feet.

Suddenly he was just there, with one arm draped around her, and his body leaning un-steadily against hers. And yet he seemed curiously weightless . . . so very light to carry . . .

Later, when she tried to remember it, it would seem almost like a dream—how they'd managed that slow and tedious walk together through the cemetery.

As though time had magically suspended until the exact second she felt those wooden stairs beneath her feet and suddenly realized that the two of them were safe inside the hiding place.

She guided him to the farthest corner—a practically invisible spot behind some old trunks and suitcases—then eased him to the floor. To her relief the makeshift bandage seemed to be holding, so she decided to leave it for now. It was still inconceivable to her that he could even be alive. He must have superhuman strength to have lasted this long.

But he hasn't completely survived . . . not yet.

Quickly she began making a mental list. She'd have to bring food and water—no doubt he was badly dehydrated. And she'd have to bring clothes—his were soaked with blood. A pillow, blankets, first-aid kit, though she had no idea what difference any of that could possibly make in the shape he was in. Splints and stitches seemed useless—hopeless even—but she could at least clean him with antiseptics and bandage him, give him something for the pain. She had the medicine Dr. Fielding had prescribed for her after the accident—between that and all the drugs Irene took on a regular basis, there was sure to be something that would help.

It amazed her, really. How much calmer she was beginning to feel now, even though the situation was still so critical and so very surreal. She wouldn't let herself consider the probable outcome or how she'd be forced to deal with it. Better to believe that there would be time later for all the questions she needed to ask, all the answers she needed to know. Better to focus right now on making him feel comfortable and cared for and safe.

Gathering all the drop cloths she could find, Lucy took them outside and shook them. She used some soiled rags to wipe dust and cobwebs from the corner. Then she spread one of the drop cloths on the floor, emptied out the bags of old clothes, arranged them into a pallet, and topped them with another large cloth. The crude bed smelled of mildew, but at least it was thick and relatively soft. Until she could bring supplies, it would have to do.

As Lucy moved back to survey her work, she realized the young man was watching her. He was half lying, half sitting against the wall where she'd left him, but she'd been so involved in what she was doing, she hadn't been paying attention. His stare was fixed, his eyes glazed. She reached over and felt his brow.

"What's your name?" she asked gently.

His lips moved in a soundless response. As Lucy leaned in closer, he tried again.

Jared? Had he said Jared?

"Jared," she repeated softly.

His stare didn't waver. His eyes didn't blink.

"I want you to rest now," Lucy soothed him. "I want you to try to sleep while I go home for a while."

Could he even hear her? Was he past the point of understanding?

"You'll be okay here. I'll come back as soon as I can, and I won't tell anyone about you. I promise."

She thought he might have attempted a nod. Very carefully she lowered him onto the pallet, then piled more layers of drop cloths on top of him. She wouldn't bother with his clothes right now, not till she had fresh ones to replace them with. In the meantime, she prayed he'd be warm enough.

She started to reassure him again, but saw he was sleeping—either that or he was blessedly unconscious. She felt his forehead, then lifted his left hand to place it under the covers. The sleeve of his jacket had worked partway up his arm, revealing long, taut ridges of vein . . . sinewy cords of muscle . . . scars and calluses of hard work. And something else she hadn't noticed before.

It looked like a tattoo.

Or . . . what was left of one.

At some time there had been an intricate design, only now it was practically obliterated by the puckered remains of a burn. The scar was large—much wider than the slash on his face—and had seared into the tattoo, melting away both flesh and ink, leaving most of it illegible.

Puzzled, she bent down for a closer look.

The first thing she focused on was the snake. Or at least . . . it *appeared* to be a snake, some sort of reptilian creature, at any rate. Only half of its head was visible, and smoke seemed to be curling from its mouth. Most of the snake's body was seared away, but upon closer examination, Lucy thought it might be impaled on something—a spike, maybe, or a sword.

She ran her fingers lightly across the images, along Jared's arm. As if by touching those distorted figures, they might somehow speak to her and tell her what she longed to know.

My God . . . he could be Byron lying here . . .

Lucy checked his heartbeat one last time.

Then she climbed out of the cellar and chained the doors behind her.

6

What if he dies while you're gone?

Lucy broke all speed limits driving back to the house.

You left him there. You didn't call a doctor. You saw how bad that wound was, how dangerous, how deep. There's no way anybody could ever survive something like that. Are you out of your mind?

The Corvette squealed around a corner. Forcing herself to slow down, Lucy glanced in the rearview mirror, relieved that no other cars were behind her. The last thing she needed right now was to get stopped by the police. It was going to be hard enough sneaking into the house and gathering all the supplies she needed without Irene's knowing.

He's bound to die, and you know it. How could he not? Then what will you do with him? Leave him in the cellar? Make an anonymous phone call? Your fingerprints are all over the place. What have you gotten yourself into now?

She turned onto Lakeshore Drive, her mind spinning faster than her tires. Maybe she'd have to tell someone. Yes, she *should* tell someone. Maybe Matt. After all, he was a priest—priests *had* to keep secrets, didn't they? Wasn't that part of their job? No matter how bad those secrets might be, no matter how crazy?

You don't even know if that guy is really Byron's brother. You don't know where he's from or why he's here—he might not even know Byron at all!

Yet how could he *not* be related? With those eyes and that hair and that voice? With Byron's face gazing back at her, hovering just below the surface, like a displaced phantom?

What person in her right mind would do what you've just done? Think about it, Lucy—think about what you've done!

Lucy hit the brakes and leaned her forehead on the steering wheel. Her chest was tight; her stomach heaved in dread. She should do something. She should call for help right now. Her cell phone was right next to her, tucked inside her purse. All she had to do was dial. Jared would be taken care of—she'd never have to see him again. And if he survived, he probably wouldn't remember anything he'd said to her, anyway.

But *she* remembered.

"Please . . . for Byron's sake . . ."

That's why she was doing this.

Even though it made no sense, even though she wasn't sure she even believed him, she would do what Jared asked of her.

For Byron's sake.

Lifting her head, Lucy took a deep breath and started off again. Past all the homes of the rich and privileged. Past the sweeping lawns and tennis courts and four-car garages, until at last she reached Irene's street.

As she neared the house, Lucy's heart plunged to her toes. What looked like a police car was parked in front, and she could see her aunt and a bulky man in uniform talking together at the front door.

Oh no . . . now what?

For a moment, she couldn't even move.

Her first thought was that someone had

discovered Jared lying in the church cellar.

Her second thought was that Irene would glance down at any second and discover the headstone hidden in the shrubs beside the porch.

Lucy's hands were slick with sweat. She tightened her grip on the steering wheel and tried to stay calm. From the serious look on Irene's face, something was definitely wrong, and Lucy's mind struggled for an answer.

Angela? Had the search for Angela come to a tragic end? Or was it something else—some other bad surprise that would once again turn Lucy's world upside down?

But she couldn't escape now—she'd already been seen. She swung the car into the driveway. The man in uniform had turned to stare at her, and Irene was waving at her to get out of the car.

Lucy took a deep breath. Like a robot, she turned off the engine and opened the door. Even from here she could see how grave the man's expression was, how tightly Irene's hands were clasped together. Why wasn't anybody saying anything? What was going on?

Nervously, she shut the car door. She started around the front of the Corvette, then froze as she caught sight of her shoes.

With all she'd had to deal with this morning, there'd been no time to think about her appearance or the alarm it was sure to cause. She'd cleaned up a little before leaving the cellar, but now she stared in horror at her bloodstained clothes and hands, realizing there was probably blood on her face, as well. Her sweater and scarf were missing. Her coat was gone. She looked like she'd come from a slaughterhouse.

I can't let them see me like this. What am I going to say?

As her aunt's gestures grew more insistent, Lucy began walking again. By the time she reached the front door, she'd managed to come up with a few lame excuses that she quickly blurted out.

"I'm okay, but there was an accident."

Irene's spine slowly stiffened. "An accident? While you were driving?"

"No. Not a car accident."

"Then *what*? Where are you hurt?"

"I'm not, I'm fine." *Sound calm, Lucy. Sound*

57

convincing. "It was someone else who got hurt, and I . . . I just tried to help."

In her customary reaction to all things emotional, Irene looked supremely annoyed. "What on earth happened?"

"I went . . . jogging."

"Jogging? With the car?"

"I used the track at school. A lot of kids go over there early to run. One of the girls fell on some broken glass."

Lucy could feel two pairs of eyes raking her over. She managed an apologetic smile.

"Her cuts were pretty deep—a few of us finally got the bleeding stopped, but it took a while. And she was shivering so bad, I just gave her some of my clothes."

The brawny cop hadn't said a word. He stared at Lucy with a neutral expression and blocked her way inside. After a tense pause, Irene finally nodded.

"This is Sheriff Stark, Lucy. He wants to talk with you."

"With me?" Lucy's heart plummeted again. "Well, I really have to get ready for school—"

"This won't take long," the sheriff assured her.

Hugging herself, Lucy looked up at him with innocent concern. "Okay. Sure. What do you need?"

"It might be more comfortable if we all go inside."

Irene hadn't moved from the doorway. From the way she was regarding Sheriff Stark, it was clear she found the intrusion offensive. "As I said before, Presley, I fail to see the purpose of any of this."

Lucy glanced from her aunt to the officer. Her stomach was churning again, and she was starting to feel faint. Whatever this was, it couldn't possibly be good. Whatever this was, it could only mean delay and disaster for Jared.

"Well, you know how it is," Sheriff Stark said smoothly. "Just trying to do my job."

He stepped aside to let Lucy pass. Irene led the way to the living room and motioned them all to sit down.

"So, Lucy." The sheriff was smiling at her now. A forced, practiced smile that wasn't the least bit sincere. "First off, don't feel like you're being singled out. We'll be interviewing all the Pine Ridge students over the next few days."

59

Nodding, Lucy shifted uneasily in her chair. She knew she should understand what he was talking about, but her mind had gone totally blank.

"I just want to ask you a few questions," the sheriff continued.

Again she nodded, returning his smile for good measure.

"How well did you know Wanda Carver?"

The smile froze on her lips. What was this about? Why was he asking her about Wanda Carver?

Lucy thought a moment, then heard herself answer, "Not well. Just from school."

"So you weren't a close friend of hers?"

"No."

"Didn't hang out with her or anything like that?"

Lucy shook her head.

"But you did *know* her." A statement, not a question. The sheriff fixed her with a level stare.

"Well . . . I knew who she was."

"This is ridiculous," Irene fumed. "I don't see how any of this could possibly be beneficial—"

"Irene, please," Sheriff Stark cut in.

Silence filled the room. An uncomfortable silence that settled heavily on Lucy's shoulders. She watched the sheriff lean toward her and clasp his beefy hands between his knees. "Lucy, did you have any contact with Wanda Carver on Wednesday?"

Lucy gazed back at him. Contact with Wanda Carver? Her mind flashed a picture of the girl's face, then went vague and confused. She had to get back to the church, back to Jared in the cellar. From some far-off place she wondered if she looked as dazed as she felt.

"I . . ." She had to think a minute. She had to try to remember. "I saw her in the hall at school."

"And what happened?"

"Happened?" It was obvious Sheriff Stark was after something—dropping hints and expecting some sort of response. Lucy glanced over at her aunt, but she read nothing in those flint-gray eyes. "Nothing happened. She gave me a flyer."

"A flyer?"

"Information about the candlelight vigil. For Angela."

"And then what happened?"

"I went to class."

"And did you *say* anything to Wanda? *Before* you went to class?"

Lucy felt trapped. Why was the sheriff so interested in what she'd said to Wanda that day? How did he even know about it? And what made the event so important that he'd come here to the house to ask her about it?

"Do you remember, Lucy?"

But it was all getting clearer now. Running back to Wanda, warning the girl to be careful. Feeling so foolish about it, but still taking the chance. Feeling responsible somehow. *Wishing Wanda had listened . . .*

Wishing I'd never had that vision.

Lucy's mouth was dry. She ran her tongue slowly over her lips.

"Lucy," the sheriff said, "there are some stories going around. Now, I know how rumors get started and how they can get out of hand. But some kids are saying you threatened Wanda Carver that day before she died."

All the blood drained from Lucy's face. She held on tightly to the arms of her chair.

"Threatened her? What are you talking about?"

"This is outrageous," Irene said. "I think this interrogation has gone far enough."

But the sheriff lifted a restraining hand. "Irene, a young girl has been murdered, and—"

"Murdered!"

Had *she* gasped out the word, Lucy wondered, or had Aunt Irene? Or maybe they *both* had, Lucy decided, because Irene was looking every bit as shocked now as Lucy was feeling.

Murder?

The living room walls seemed to tilt and sway as her brain struggled desperately to compute. Even Irene's composure had temporarily faltered—Lucy could see her aunt staring at the floor and fingering her expensive pearls with quivering fingers.

"Murdered?" Lucy choked out at last. "But . . . but . . . no—she had an accident! That's what the police said last night—that Wanda had an *accident*."

"Well, the thing is, I don't believe we ever *officially* called it an accident," the sheriff said.

Lucy's mind raced backward—back to the

candlelight vigil, to the unexpected arrival of the police, the shocked faces of the students, back to Dakota's stunned and sad announcement.

"She fell off the footbridge over that old drainage ditch in the park. She broke her neck on the concrete."

"But it *must* have been an accident," Lucy murmured. A chill traced up the length of her spine, and it was getting harder and harder to keep her voice steady. "Why would you think anything else? Why would you think it was murder?"

"I'm afraid that's confidential."

"But why are you asking *me* about it?"

"We're talking to everyone who knew Wanda. Just trying to gather as much information as we can."

At this Irene came to life again, planting herself between Lucy and their unwelcome visitor, fixing him with an icy stare.

"You're entirely mistaken about all this, Presley. You, of all people, should know that brutal crimes never happen in Pine Ridge."

"I know you'd like to believe that," the sheriff answered gently. "On account of Angela and all.

And you're right—we've never had those kinds of crimes here before." Pausing, he rubbed his forehead, then cast her a reluctant glance. "But we have now."

Lucy's throat was closing up. She tried to take a deep breath, but the air had gone thick and sour.

The stranger who was in the mausoleum, covered with blood . . .

"So what about these rumors, Lucy?" The sheriff's voice bullied its way into her brain. "*Did* you threaten Wanda Carver the day before she died?"

The stranger I tried to help . . . the stranger I hid in the church cellar . . .

"Oh, for heaven's sake!" Irene was furiously indignant. "Surely you don't think Lucy had anything to do with this! I've never heard anything so—"

"Why don't we just let Lucy tell us. I'm sure she has a reasonable explanation."

Reasonable? Oh, right, Sheriff, I bumped into Wanda Carver and got slammed with a supernatural vision.

For an instant, Lucy stifled a wild urge to

laugh. No matter what she said, it wouldn't sound reasonable. No matter how honest she was, he wouldn't believe her. Only Byron understood. And she doubted very much that Byron would suddenly appear to help her out.

"It was a dream," she said solemnly. "I had a dream about Wanda Carver. And it was so real, it scared me."

Sheriff Stark looked blank. "A dream."

"Yes."

"So . . . what happened in this dream?"

"I'm not sure. I mean . . . it was all mixed up, but in the dream, I knew Wanda was falling."

"Falling? How? From what?"

"I don't know. That part wasn't clear."

"You just said it was real to you."

"It *was* real. But not like whole scenes. More like images blinking on and off. Weird feelings and sensations." *And the fact that Wanda would die. And the* date *that Wanda would die . . .*

"And when did you have the dream?"

"Not then. I mean, it was days before that. But it just stayed with me—I couldn't forget about it. So I finally said something to her."

"And that's when you threatened her."

66

"No." Lucy was determined to hold his gaze. "I never threatened her. I just told her to be careful."

Another uneasy silence fell between them. The sheriff lowered his head and stroked his chin. Stared down at the floor for several moments. Looked at her again.

"So that's what Wanda's friends heard—you telling her to be careful?"

"I felt stupid about it. I mean, I didn't even know her, and I figured she'd think I was crazy, and then she'd tell the whole school. And it *didn't* make sense, not even to me. But . . . but I couldn't let it go. I had to tell her."

"And that's all you said?"

Lucy nodded.

"And nothing happened previously between you and Wanda? An argument, maybe? Problems with a boyfriend? Problems in class?"

"I told you. I hardly knew her."

"Presley." Irene's frosty tone demanded his attention. "You helped search for my niece recently when she went missing."

Sheriff Stark nodded.

"Then I'm sure you can appreciate the

severe trauma Lucy's suffered since her disappearance."

"I know she's been seeing Dr. Fielding, yes."

"And are you aware of the various ways that trauma can manifest? Depression? Amnesia? Severe nightmares . . . not to mention the possibility of hallucinations?"

The sheriff kept quiet.

"I'm sure Dr. Fielding will be more than happy to review Lucy's medical records with you. I'll willingly give my permission, and have my attorney sit in on your discussion."

Sheriff Stark obviously had sense enough to recognize Irene's limits. As a slow flush spread over his face, he shook his head politely and got up.

"No need for that, Irene. You've been more than cooperative. You, too, young lady. Thank you both for your time."

Miserably, Lucy watched Irene escort the sheriff to the door. She wished her aunt hadn't gone into quite so much detail about post-traumatic stress syndrome. Amnesia? Hallucinations? If anything else remotely suspicious *ever* happened in Pine Ridge, Lucy would be the first suspect on Sheriff Stark's list.

Still, she had to admire her aunt's protectiveness. In spite of the circumstances, it made Lucy feel good that Irene had rushed to defend her. She even smiled appreciatively as her aunt came back to the living room and regarded her with a long, appraising stare.

"What on earth were you thinking, Lucy?" Irene demanded.

Shocked, Lucy watched the stare harden into a cold frown of disapproval.

"Do you have any idea of the problems you've caused? Did you even *consider* how this was going to look?" Irene marched to the opposite wall and straightened an oil painting that didn't need straightening. "Is it because you want attention? Because you're new at school and feel a need to fit in?"

"I . . . I don't understand—"

"There are more *normal* ways of fitting in, you know. You don't need some bizarre identity in order to feel special."

"Aunt Irene—"

"No wonder Wanda Carver's friends thought you were threatening her. Walking up like that, telling her to be careful—and all because of some dream? I suppose the next thing you're going to tell me is that you read minds."

A knot of hurt and anger welled up inside Lucy, bringing tears to her eyes. "It was real," she said flatly.

"It was a dream. And dreams are *not* real. Dreams are simply bits and pieces of our subconscious—things we encounter during the ordinary course of a day. People we see, dialogue on television. Anti-anxiety pills and upset stomachs."

Lucy felt beaten down, too tired to answer. She lowered her eyes as the lecture continued.

"I'm sure the whole neighborhood saw the sheriff's car in my driveway. The whole *town* will know about it by this evening."

And then those final words as Irene turned to leave for work.

"Perhaps you came home from the hospital too soon, Lucy. It might be better for you to go somewhere else for a while. Somewhere peaceful . . . and private. For a nice long rest."

7

Irene wasn't serious, Lucy kept telling herself.

Those comments about peace and privacy and nice long rests—surely Lucy had misunderstood. Those comments that made her think of being sent away to another strange place and shoved out of sight in another strange room . . .

She didn't mean anything. She was just upset.

And Lucy didn't have time to agonize over it now.

As soon as Irene left, she washed her hands, changed her clothes, then began a mad sweep through the house, taking blankets and towels, gathering clothes from closets and what food she could find in the kitchen. There was a thermos in the pantry. A bottle of brandy in the dining room sideboard. Flashlights from her nightstand and the coat closet, a battery-operated lantern from the garage, sedatives and first-aid supplies from the medicine cabinet, and a nearly full carafe of French Roast in the automatic coffeemaker. She mixed the brandy with the coffee and made old-cheese-and-stale-croissant sandwiches. Once she had everything together, she stuffed as much as she could into her backpack and carried the rest. Then, grabbing a jacket on her way out, she threw everything into the trunk of the car and headed back to the church.

You'll never get away with this.

Lucy's eyes darted back and forth between the street ahead and her rearview mirror. She was breaking speed limits again, and she couldn't afford to get pulled over. She'd have to come up with some excuse for skipping school. Irene was sure to find out about it—as if Lucy wasn't treading on thin enough ice already.

You'll never get away with this, hiding that guy in the cellar, taking care of him all by yourself. If he dies— and he probably will—it'll be you *who killed him. That is . . . if he doesn't end up killing you first . . .*

"Oh God," Lucy whispered to herself. "I'm in so much trouble."

He *couldn't* be a killer, could he? Mysterious, yes . . . a little scary, even . . . but a *killer*?

Lucy wished she knew exactly what had happened to Wanda Carver. Knowing details about the so-called murder might help her figure out this crazy predicament she was in, who Jared really was.

And what if he is a killer? Would you just leave him there to die?

In spite of her better judgment, Lucy knew she wouldn't—she'd never willingly abandon anyone in need. Even if she ended up calling someone to help her. Turning the whole thing over to the authorities, letting somebody else handle all her weird, creepy problems for a change.

Byron's brother . . .

Leaning forward, Lucy stepped on the gas. She sped past a delivery van and was practically through an intersection before she even saw the stop sign.

"Damn!"

The whole car shuddered as she hit the

brakes. Several horns honked their annoyance, but she stared straight in front of her and tried to stay focused.

The truth is, I don't really know who *he is. He could be* anybody. *He could be an escaped lunatic. An escaped convict. He could be some homeless guy who got bitten by a very large, very mean dog while he was trying to break into somebody's house.*

Another horn blared, ordering her to go. Lucy floored the accelerator and took the next corner too sharply, hitting a patch of ice and sliding several feet before she finally got the car under control. Shaking badly, she swerved into the first parking lot she could find. Then she turned off the engine and lowered her head onto the steering wheel.

It was only eight-thirty, but the day—like so many others in her life lately—had already turned disastrous. She closed her eyes and thought back . . . to her vision of Wanda Carver . . . to the touch of Jared's hand. Surely she would have *glimpsed* something evil, *felt* something horrible, gotten some unmistakable sign if he'd been involved in Wanda's murder.

Blood . . . screams . . . burning . . .

But like all her other visions, no clear pictures, no definite meanings . . .

Pain . . . surrender . . . pleasure . . .

Why couldn't she see further? And why—despite some violent images—was she sensing somehow that Jared had no fatal connections to Wanda Carver?

Because that's what you want to believe?

Lucy's breathing slowed. For an instant she saw Jared again, piercingly vivid, almost as though he were sitting beside her now. The handsome stranger with the amber eyes and tousled hair, with that desperate expression as he'd begged her for help . . .

He *couldn't* be a murderer, Lucy told herself.

You don't want *him to be a murderer.*

"Lucy!"

Eyes flying open, Lucy nearly jumped out of her skin. She hadn't heard anyone approaching the car, but now she saw a familiar face pressed against her window.

"Lucy, what are you doing here?"

As Dakota peered in at her, Lucy couldn't help feeling a twinge of guilt. She still remembered the way Dakota had looked at her last night, after Wanda Carver's body had been discovered. *"They're saying it happened sometime early this morning,"* Dakota had said. *"But then . . . you already knew that, didn't you?"*

And Lucy hadn't answered, hadn't said a word. She'd just turned and run away, leaving her friend behind and feeling like the worst kind of liar.

She felt ashamed of herself, even now.

She hesitated a second, then rolled down the window.

"I thought that was you," Dakota said matter-of-factly. "How come you're not at school?"

She was wearing camouflage pants, a white jacket made of curly fake fur, and a red plaid hunting cap with earflaps. Her multicolored scarf was twisted around her neck and hanging down her back, and at the moment, it appeared to be sparkling. Lucy realized it was covered with gold glitter.

"I . . ." Lucy stammered, "I . . . how come *you're* not?"

"Doughnuts." Dakota lifted a stack of large, flat boxes so Lucy could see. "I think they're supposed to lull us into a false sense of security." When Lucy didn't respond, she added, "Father

76

Matt sent me to get them. For the interviews. What's that on your face?"

Lucy's hand went immediately to her cheek. She scrunched down in her coat as Dakota leaned toward her.

"It looks like blood." Dakota frowned. "Are you hurt?"

"No, I . . . fell . . . someone—"

"You *fell* on someone?"

"No." What was it she'd told the sheriff earlier? Lucy couldn't remember now—all she could think about was getting away from here and getting back to the church. "I know about Wanda," she blurted out. "About it not being an accident."

She made herself meet Dakota's eyes. She thought once more about what Dakota had said to her after the discovery of Wanda's body— *"But then . . . you already knew that, didn't you?"*— and she braced herself for the questions and accusations she felt sure would come.

But there was no curiosity in Dakota's eyes, only that same open acceptance as before. And all Dakota said now was, "Is that why you ran away last night?"

77

"No." Lucy shook her head. For one quick moment she actually felt disappointed. For one quick moment she almost wished Dakota *would* confront her. "I didn't know anything about a murder then. Look, Dakota—"

"Well, I guess everyone knows by now. Small town. Front page of the paper."

"I haven't seen the paper." Reality was tugging her back again. She had to get back to the church—she had to hurry—*hurry!* But Dakota wasn't moving, so Lucy added, "Sheriff Stark was at the house this morning."

"Oh. He's a good friend of your aunt's, right?" Dakota didn't wait for Lucy to answer. "He's at school today, too. Everyone's scared and really upset—they can't believe another tragedy's happened. The police want to interview every single student. Behind closed doors, one at a time. So I guess you won't have to go through that."

"The visit wasn't about sparing me; it was a courtesy to Irene. Heaven forbid her glorious reputation should be smeared. They wouldn't dare arrest me in public."

"What do you mean, arrest you?"

"I mean . . ." Lucy's words trailed off help-lessly. She reached out and touched her friend's sleeve. "Oh, Dakota—"

"What's wrong?" The expression on Dakota's face softened, a knowing and genuine concern. It was all Lucy could do not to open her heart and spill everything out. "Lucy, what is it?"

Not now! There's no time! Hurry!

"It's . . ." But somehow Lucy held back. Somehow she collected herself and squeezed all her emotions into a guilty frown. "About last night, I know I owe you an explanation—"

"You don't owe me anything."

Dakota, I want to tell you, but I'm afraid! "Yes. Yes, I do." *I need to tell you, but I'm all confused about things, and I don't want you to get hurt!* "What you said to me—"

"I wasn't trying to put you on the spot. It was an observation."

"And why I went back to Wanda that day in the hall—" Lucy couldn't help it, she was starting to babble. If she didn't get out of here soon, she was going to explode.

"You don't owe me anything," Dakota assured her again. "But there's more blood here on your hand, and I just want to make sure you're okay."

Tears stung Lucy's eyes. "I don't know. For now, yes, I think I'm okay. But I need to talk to you. Later. Where no one can hear us."

Nodding, Dakota slowly drew back. "Are you coming to school?"

"I can't right now."

"Okay. I can call the office if you want. I'm pretty good at imitating your aunt's voice," Dakota mimicked, just to prove it. "I can say you're sick."

In spite of herself, Lucy almost laughed. "And if they catch you, you'll get suspended. I'll try to come in later. No use both of us being in trouble."

"Did you eat this morning? You look really pale; maybe you should eat." Dakota's voice returned to normal. "Father Matt thinks we'll all cooperate with the police more if we're eating. Thus"—once again she displayed her boxes—"doughnuts."

The mere suggestion of eating right now made Lucy feel sicker. She started up the engine again and managed a halfhearted wave.

But Dakota wasn't watching. The girl's head

was tilted back, her eyes sweeping over the cold dead sky. And Lucy was suddenly very much afraid.

"You sense it, too, don't you?" Dakota murmured. "Something in the air today. Something bad and dark, that's never been there before. Like the whole town's suddenly changed. And that bad thing is waiting. And nobody feels it but us."

Lucy followed the direction of her friend's gaze. Drawing a slow, shaky breath, she spoke with more conviction than she felt.

"It's just grief, I think. And also shock. Because . . . you know what people say . . . murders never happen in Pine Ridge."

"Well . . ." Dakota gave an odd little smile. "At least none they know about."

8

There *was* an eerie feeling in the air.

As Lucy made her way slowly through the graveyard, she couldn't help shivering—not only from the cold, but also from Dakota's unsettling prophecy. Her ears strained for each subtle sound; her eyes glanced keenly in every direction. But this section of Pine Ridge Cemetery seemed more silent and remote than ever.

The fog of early morning had been replaced by snow. Raw wind sliced between the headstones, and a pewter sky was darkening quickly to the north.

Unconsciously Lucy quickened her pace. She'd had to park the car behind the cemetery and away from prying eyes, which meant a longer, more difficult walk to the church. She felt fairly confident no one would be out here today, but she didn't dare take a chance on being seen. The weight of her backpack made her clumsy. She kept her head down, ducking for cover between lopsided markers and broken statues, using the blankets she carried to block the wind. And she wondered what she was going to do once she got to the hiding place.

What if Jared's dead? What if he's not there at all? What if someone passing on the street in front happens to notice me?

Lucy knew if she thought any more about it, she might lose her nerve completely. She checked her surroundings one last time, braced herself for the unknown, and made a beeline for the cellar.

It took several minutes to loosen the chain, another few minutes of struggling to pull open the heavy doors. Taking a flashlight from her pocket, she squatted on the top step and shone the light down, guiding it slowly from wall to wall.

Something moved.

Without warning, something dark and shapeless jerked back from the beam of her flashlight and vanished into the shadows.

A scream caught in Lucy's throat. Whatever had moved, had moved quickly; she hadn't been able to make out a single detail. In fact, as her brain struggled to compute, she wasn't entirely convinced that it *hadn't* been a shadow after all, just one among many, distorted by the sudden burst of her flashlight and the gray flitter of snow through the opening behind her.

"Hello?" she called softly.

Whatever she thought she'd seen, it wasn't moving now. The cellar was as quiet as a grave.

"Jared, are you here?"

She held her breath to listen.

She could hear the tripping of her heart, but nothing else. Her grip began to tighten on the flashlight.

"It's me. Lucy. I came alone, like I promised."

Was that a draft of wind she'd felt just now? Like an icy hand wrapping slowly around her ankle? She gasped and lost her footing, sliding down several steps and dropping the flashlight. As she flung out both arms to catch herself, a sliver of wood gouged deep into the palm of her right hand.

Lucy cried out, from surprise as well as pain. The blankets tumbled down the stairs, and the flashlight rolled across the floor, its single ray skipping over a pile of bloody clothes.

"Shut the doors," Jared said softly.

Despite the sudden chill up her spine, Lucy managed to keep her voice steady. "Where are you?"

"Please don't look at me."

She hesitated, unsure what to do. Then she reached up and drew down the doors, plunging the cellar into darkness.

It took several minutes for her eyes to adjust. The flashlight had finally come to a stop, angled directly into a corner, and as Lucy picked it up, she couldn't help but follow the direction of the light.

Jared was lying there, watching her.

Lying on the bed where she'd left him, except that the improvised bandages were gone, discarded with other blood-soaked belongings in that dirty heap on the floor. He wore only jeans now, low and tight around his hips, and still damp with his blood.

Something's not right.

Lucy gazed at him in confusion.

She could see the gauntness of his face, the tight clench of his jaws, the feverish glow in his eyes. Sweat shone on his bare chest and along his brow.

She shifted the beam of her flashlight.

The burned tattoo on his arm stood out in sharp relief against his skin—but not *pale* skin, Lucy realized with a shock—not that ghostly white pallor of death he'd had before.

"Don't do this," he whispered. "Turn away."

But she *couldn't* turn away, any more than she could keep herself from lowering the flashlight and redirecting its beam onto his wound.

His wound . . .

The light shook in Lucy's hand. It settled on the left side of Jared's body, and she stared in utter disbelief.

His wound had grown smaller.

Where a raw, bloody hole had gaped so hideously before, now small sections of flesh appeared to be shrinking and closing up. Protruding bones seemed to have pulled back toward the shattered rib cage. And the skin, hanging in hopelessly tattered shreds, actually looked as though it were starting to reattach.

"My God . . ."

The flashlight clattered to the floor. As if from some far and distant place, Jared's words reached out to her.

"It's not complete yet, Lucy. The pain won't stop till then."

"No. No . . . it's impossible . . ."

She wasn't conscious of backing up . . . of stumbling over her own feet as she tried to escape. But suddenly there were voices—voices coming from outside—and Lucy froze, halfway up the stairs.

"I *know* I saw someone!" a woman insisted.

Lucy recognized her voice at once. Mrs. Dempsey.

"Just as I got here for work—just as I parked my car! I'm telling you, I *didn't* imagine it! Someone was sneaking around behind the church!"

"Do you have any idea where they went?" a man asked.

Mrs. Dempsey sounded indignant. "How in heaven's name should I know that? But there's some crazy murderer running around Pine

Ridge, and I want you to check out *every inch* of this place!"

Lucy didn't see the swift movement behind her. She didn't even have time to react as the hand clamped over her mouth, as she felt herself being half lifted, half dragged back into the corner.

She tried to struggle, but only for a second.

Only till Jared's whispered warning in her ear.

"I don't want trouble. Stay still and keep down."

The flashlight snapped off. Jared pulled her to the floor as the cellar doors flung open.

"Someone must be in here!" Mrs. Dempsey exclaimed. "See? Just look at this chain!"

A brilliant beam of light swept around them, over walls and ceiling, arcing above their heads. *Help so close, and yet so far away.* Lucy wanted to yell, to break free, but she was pressed so close against him, and he was holding her so tight. She could feel his bare chest . . . his breath on her neck. His arms were surprisingly strong.

"Well if there *was* someone here, there's no one here now," the man announced. "Look, Mrs. Dempsey, you better get inside now— this snow's really coming down."

"As if I'll have any peace!" the woman fumed. "I've got my cleaning to do—I can't be worrying about some maniac breaking in and throwing me down the basement steps!"

"Well, lock yourself inside the church—*no* one could break through those doors. I'll put this chain on good and tight, but you'd better get a padlock, just to be sure."

No! Lucy's hopes sank. Once more she tried to pull away, but again found it impossible. She could hear the chain being secured on the outside doors; she could hear the voices arguing, then fading off.

Time hung suspended in the darkness. Thoughts of death and murder spun crazily through her brain. The air in the cellar was much too warm, squeezing her, suffocating her, Jared's skin so hot with fever, Jared's lips burning as they lowered to her hair . . .

It seemed an eternity that he held her. An eternity before he finally whispered to her again.

"When I let you go, you'll be very quiet. You won't scream. And you won't tell anyone I'm here. Understood?"

Lucy nodded. There was a razor-sharp edge

beneath his soft-spoken words. And a faint but unmistakable quiver that he was struggling hard to conceal.

"I didn't intend to scare you," he added, almost grudgingly.

At last Lucy was able to move. She pulled away and put distance between them as he retreated into the shadows.

There's another door in here.

She'd seen it earlier, camouflaged between some shelves, along one of these walls. She hadn't been able to open it before, but maybe— if she moved fast enough, if she could somehow break it down . . .

She dove headlong through the darkness. But instead of finding a way out, she found herself immediately trapped in Jared's arms.

"If you're looking for that door," he said, "you have a terrible sense of direction."

9

There was no force this time.

Lucy's captivity lasted only a moment before Jared released her.

It had nothing to do with courtesy or consideration, she was quick to realize—but because his strength was rapidly giving out. She could feel his exhaustion, the weakening of his grip. And in the silence of the cellar, his breathing was ragged with pain.

"It's not complete yet . . . The pain won't stop till then."

Jared's words sounded clearly in her head, though she knew he hadn't spoken aloud since letting her go. She began backing away from him again, then stopped abruptly, overcome with confusion and fear.

How had he known she would bolt for that

locked door? She hadn't even known it herself until the last possible second. How had he seen her in the dark? How had he caught her so fast?

Without warning the flashlight came on. The bright glare caught her full in the face, and she put up both hands, trying to shield her eyes. She felt like a deer trapped in headlights. And suddenly, the fact that he would put her at such a deliberate disadvantage made her furious.

"Turn that off!"

Lucy swung out blindly, sending the flashlight into a wall. With a weird sense of satisfaction, she heard plastic smashing apart.

"Why?" she demanded. "Why are you doing this?"

His answer was a long and guarded silence.

She couldn't see him, couldn't see *anything* except lingering pinpoints of light, but she stepped forward and threw out a challenge.

"I can wait just as long as you can. But we'll do it on equal ground."

Again the silence. A silence so lengthy that Lucy felt compelled to speak again.

"What is this anyway? Some kind of sick joke?"

Why wouldn't he answer her? Why wouldn't

he talk? Her head felt as if it was going to explode.

And then she sensed a stirring in the shadows. A calm presence . . . and curious . . . and much nearer than she'd expected.

"Why would you think it's a joke?" Jared asked softly.

"Why? Well, why *not*? I see the looks at school—I hear the rumors. It's not like I don't know what's going on."

"What *is* going on?"

"Things! Things that just happen to me!" The words burst out before Lucy even realized. She hesitated, unsure of what she'd just said, and unsure of why she'd said it.

His voice gave her a solemn prompting. "Tell me about those things."

"Things," Lucy said, evasive now as she stared through the dark at his question. *Crazy things like wounds healing all by themselves.* But out loud she added, "Things that nobody would ever believe. Unless those things really *were* jokes."

There was no response from Jared this time. Lucy forced a harsh and humorless laugh.

"So if this really *is* some kind of trick you're playing," she said bitterly, "let me set the record straight once and for all. I'm just as sad about Byron as you are—probably even more. I feel guilty every single day, because he died and I didn't. I wish I'd never come to this stupid town. I wish I'd never met Byron. I'd give *anything* if things could be different. I'd leave here in a second if I had some other place to go, but I don't. So please. You've had your fun. Just leave me alone."

She wouldn't give him the satisfaction of seeing her cry. She faced the shadows defiantly, but they seemed to be empty now.

Jared was standing right next to her.

His whisper caressed her like velvet.

"I'm not who you think I am, Lucy. And if you were mine . . . I'd never leave you alone."

A shiver went through her, languid and warm.

His fingers closed around hers.

"Let me see your hand," he said.

"What?" Lucy felt strangely disoriented. She was still angry, still determined—hadn't she made that clear? He was supposed to be letting her go now, but he wasn't. She was pushing him away, but he was getting closer.

"Your hand—it's still bleeding. Let me see it."

Still bleeding? She'd completely forgotten about falling on the stairs. But as Jared spread her fingers and pressed his lips against her palm, it wasn't the nasty scrape there that made her cry out.

Lucy clutched at her chest.

The pain was so intense, she couldn't bear it. It was as though her heart were being pierced— rendered in half—sliced straight through with a keen, swift blade. And then, just as quickly as it had struck, the anguish was gone again, leaving her breathless and shaken.

"It's a very deep splinter," Jared was saying. "It'll have to come out."

Lucy stared at him in amazement. Couldn't he see how she was trembling? Hadn't he seen what just happened? Wasn't he the least bit concerned?

It did really happen . . . didn't it?

"Jared—" she began, then broke off with a gasp.

His mouth was warm against her palm. She felt the splinter shift slightly beneath her skin . . . the effortless glide of it through her flesh, as Jared drew the splinter out.

"That's a very interesting scar," he whispered.

She wanted to give him an answer—something believable and acceptable that he would never recall again. But her mind had gone hazy, and her eyes had drifted shut. Darkness flowed over her, but she wasn't afraid. She knew she was awake, yet she seemed to be dreaming.

A trickle of blood on my hand . . .

Blood being kissed away . . .

"A girl was killed last night," Lucy whispered, and like before, she wasn't quite sure why she'd brought this up. It was such an effort to talk now. Her hand was throbbing, and her body felt flushed. Her pulse beat much too slow. "I can't stop thinking about it. I keep imagining how scared she must have been."

Silence stretched around her. When Jared finally spoke, his voice was low and emotionless.

"Maybe there wasn't time for her to be scared."

"But it was dark. And she was all alone."

"Yes," he murmured. "I know."

10

She dreamed she was in a storm.

A winter storm so fierce and cold that it was turning her into a solid block of ice. She could feel her limbs freezing, inch by inch . . . her hands . . . even her lips . . . until she couldn't struggle anymore, couldn't even scream for help. And yet there *was* help close by, searchers with dogs, trying to find her, calling her name, walking slowly past her and leaving her buried in the snow . . .

"I'm here!" Lucy screamed a silent scream. "Please don't let me die!"

She could hear their footsteps crunching over the frozen ground; she could smell the damp, musky fur of the dogs. Someone fired a gun— one single muffled shot—and then the whole world went white and still.

Lucy's eyes flew open.

There was no white world around her now, only black, murky shadows. She was gasping for breath, and her mind scrambled furiously, trying to make sense of where she was. Still trapped in a nightmare? The cave in the woods? Her bedroom at Aunt Irene's?

Every instinct warned her to escape. Yet at the same time, she began to realize that something was holding her down.

A fresh wave of panic engulfed her. She was too frightened to move, but her whole body trembled uncontrollably. It took several endless seconds for the truth to sink in. And even then, the truth seeemd unbelievable.

She was lying on her side, nestled in the curve of Jared's body. His left arm was draped across her shoulder, and her forehead rested lightly on his chest. She couldn't remember how she'd gotten here, couldn't remember even falling asleep. In fact, the last thing she remembered at all was Jared pulling a splinter from her hand.

Or was that just part of my nightmare?

Her right hand was pressed to Jared's heart.

His skin was warm, and she could feel the slow, even rhythm of his breathing. But there was a vague sense of discomfort, as well—as though her palm were swollen and tender. And a lingering throb of pain kept time to Jared's heartbeat.

Lucy heard him moan. As his body shifted against her, she was able to ease out from underneath his arm. The lantern she'd brought was glowing near the bed, and the initial terror she'd felt was finally beginning to subside. She propped herself on one elbow and watched him.

She wished this *were* a joke.

Because then, in the end, there would be answers, and everything would go away, and nothing would be real.

But Lucy had no answers. And nothing had gone away except people and things she loved.

And real was *here*; real was *now*.

Just like the change in Jared.

It was obvious that his wound had healed even more. Since the last time she'd checked it, it seemed to have shrunk to nearly half its original size. No matter the weakness she'd sensed in him before, or the quiver she'd heard in his voice—now the sharp hollows of his cheeks were beginning to fill in slightly, and the bruising had practically vanished around his eyes. Even his lips looked different, Lucy thought—fuller somehow, and no longer pale. The transformation was nothing short of miraculous. Yet even though he found respite in sleep, she could tell that the pain hadn't left him. Not all of it . . . not yet.

She placed her hand gently upon his brow.

Wind . . . earth . . . sweat . . . blood . . . They drifted from his skin and from his hair, though not unpleasantly. And with them came a sense of some deep, inner struggle. Something far more desperate—more dangerous even—than a struggle for self-survival.

Lucy's fingertips slid lower, tracing the jagged mark across his face. The shock she felt was immediate and unexpected—a bolt of rage, a hatred so intense that she nearly reeled from the impact.

Alarmed, she took a closer look.

It was even deeper than she'd thought, and much more gruesome. As though something had not merely stabbed the flesh, but twisted . . .

not only cut the flesh, but slashed with relentless force.

And yet . . . he's still so beautiful . . .

Lucy gazed at him with a kind of awe.

So beautiful and so handsome, in spite of the scars.

A dark, compelling beauty, full of secrets . . .

"Stop now," she whispered to herself. "Don't go any further."

But she was already touching his arm.

Trailing her fingers lightly over the puckered skin of his burn . . . the charred remains of his tattoo . . .

This time, she cried out when the shock wave hit. As the uncontrolled fury surged through her, searing every artery and vein.

She jerked backward, clutching her fingers, shaking violently, and becoming certain of two things:

At some past time, Jared had been tortured.

And both of his scars had come from the same merciless hand.

11

She'd never expected to see such cruelty.

Such brutal anger . . . such excruciating pain.

Was it even humanly possible, she wondered, for someone to inflict—or bear—that kind of suffering?

She'd only touched Jared's scars for a moment.

How many other scars ached deep within him, far beyond her reach?

Lucy sat on the bed and watched him sleep. It was colder down here now, and she could hear the wind outside, rattling the chain on the doors. An occasional burst of snow gusted through the cracks and settled on the stairs, as if the cellar were a giant coffin and she and Jared were being buried alive.

It reminded her of the dream she'd had earlier.

She'd forgotten about it till now.

Lucy slid quietly from the bed and stood up, flexing her cramped muscles. She had no idea what time it was, or how many of her classes she'd missed so far. The office had probably already called Irene to report Lucy missing from school. She shuddered to think about it. She'd have to come up with one more really convincing excuse. Except it was getting harder and harder to keep all her excuses straight.

She glanced anxiously over at Jared. He was still sleeping, but there was a flicker of pain across his face, and she noticed a small amount of blood seeping from his wound. She found her backpack and pulled everything out. After tending to Jared as best she could, Lucy piled the blankets on him and arranged the other items within arm's reach of the bed. Then she opened the thermos of brandy-laced coffee and dropped in several sleeping pills.

"Drink this," she whispered to him. "It'll help the pain."

He seemed to understand this at some level. With his eyes still closed, he allowed her to lift his head and tip the cup to his lips.

A wave of sympathy swept through her. And then resentment and frustration. She felt sorry for Jared, and she felt sorry for herself. How could another day of her life have turned out so badly, so quickly? And how had this stranger—who looked so much like Byron—slipped into her world with such heartbreaking familiarity?

It doesn't have to be like this.

Through her turmoil of emotions, Lucy suddenly realized that one thought was trying to break through.

You could use your cell phone. When you get back to the car, use your cell phone and call for help.

It would be so easy, she knew. Just the punch of a few buttons, and then Jared and all his mysterious secrets would be out of her life forever.

You have a choice.

Lucy gazed down at Jared. From his peaceful expression she could tell that the drugs and brandy were already working. He looked younger somehow. Innocent. And suddenly, helplessly vulnerable.

"Damnit."

She couldn't betray him.

Not just because she'd given her word. Or because of the torments he'd suffered. Not even because of all the time and lies and worry she'd invested in him, or the veiled threats he'd made, or the way his body felt, warm and protective beside her . . .

"My choice," Lucy whispered, though she knew Jared couldn't hear her. "For Byron's sake."

12

Lucy was still determined to find a way out of the cellar.

Jared would be sleeping for quite a while; he'd be safe here and undisturbed. She'd have time to go home and clean up and try to form some kind of plan. There'd been no time today for thinking ahead. She felt amazingly lucky that she'd made it through each bizarre moment and survived.

Her whole body ached with exhaustion. She was stiff and sore from dragging Jared through the cemetery, and lugging boxes and backpacks, and falling on the stairs. There was still a faint throb in her hand. She was cold, and she was hungry. And she dreaded facing Irene when she got back to the house.

Sighing heavily, Lucy bent to pick up the lantern.

And that's when she noticed the footprints.

It didn't sink in all at once, those muddled marks upon the floor. Outlines of large shoes, and impressions of large paws, overlapping and smearing together in the dust. The prints stopped at the edge of the bed, on the side where she'd been sleeping—then seemed to reverse and trail off again in the same direction from which they'd come.

From a wall of floor-to-ceiling shelves.

And a camouflaged door.

Lucy straightened slowly, chills racing up her spine.

And once more remembered the nightmare that had woken her.

Snow and a storm and being buried alive—people searching, calling my name—the musky smell of dogs—and a gunshot . . .

Lucy kept staring at the footprints.

She tried to tell herself that she and Jared had made them, as they'd moved about the cellar. She tried to tell herself she was just imagining shoe soles and animal feet etched there in the dust, just like people could interpret cloud formations in a million different ways. After all, if something really *had* been in here, how could she not have heard? No person or animal could have been *that* quiet.

Going more cautiously now, she followed the tracks all the way back to the row of shelves. She held the lantern close to the locked door, then lowered it toward the concrete.

She was right.

The footprints had definitely started here.

They went in both directions and vanished beneath the door.

She reached out for the doorknob. She pressed her ear against the door and listened.

And something listened back.

With a sudden, horrible certainty, Lucy *felt* it—a presence poised there on the other side of that door, something *listening* just like *she* was listening.

In one instant she stumbled back; in the next, she twisted the knob and pushed with all her strength, stifling a scream as the door burst open.

The threshold was empty.

There were no footprints on the other side.

Only a long, narrow passageway with a low

ceiling and walls of crumbling brick, and what looked like a staircase rising from the shadows at the opposite end. The floor was hard-packed earth, and the dust of many years blanketed its smooth, unbroken surface.

No footprints . . .

No presence . . .

Nothing.

Lucy shut her eyes and sagged against the wall.

Nothing . . . nothing at all.

And yet *someone* had opened this door.

And someone had walked to the bed in the corner.

And as she and Jared slept in each other's arms . . . *someone* had watched.

13

She had to see where the passageway would take her.

Leaving the lantern behind, Lucy armed herself with the backpack and extra flashlight and followed the dingy corridor to its end. She had a feeling this was only one small part of the cellar, and the last thing she wanted to do was lose her way. She convinced herself there was no one watching from the closed doors and heavily banked shadows on either side—that the faint whispering was only wind seeping through cracks in the foundation. When she finally reached the staircase, she was so shaky with relief, she could barely make it up the steps.

The door at the top was unlocked. As Lucy inched it open, she found herself at the back of a closet, surrounded by spiderwebs, mouse droppings, and dead roaches. She felt too grateful to be disgusted. Holding the flashlight toward the floor, she tiptoed out onto a narrow landing, then paused to listen. The building was dark and silent; Mrs. Dempsey had obviously finished her work. Lucy had no trouble sneaking through a series of rooms and hallways until she finally came to a threshold and saw the church altar a short distance beyond.

The church altar, with Matt right beside it.

Snapping off the flashlight, Lucy drew back against the wall. Thank God she'd kept the beam angled downward; she didn't think he'd seen it. But had he heard her? She counted off seconds while she waited, but he obviously wasn't coming to investigate. Her stomach tightened as she tried to think.

Surely Matt couldn't have been in the cellar just now. Sneaking and spying and listening at doors. He would have said something, he would have offered to help. And he certainly wouldn't have had a dog with him.

What a crazy idea . . .

She chanced another look through the doorway. Candles burned on the altar, casting

111

bizarre shapes along the walls and vaulted ceiling. Matt's face was lowered, angled slightly to the right. He seemed to be studying a small object in his hands, though Lucy couldn't tell what it was. After a while he placed it on the altar and, with detached slowness, began to unfasten his priest's collar. Then he wadded up the collar, tossed it onto the altar, and turned around.

Lucy ducked back behind the corner. She could hear his footsteps moving quickly, echoing through the emptiness of the church.

He was walking straight toward her.

Still as a statue, she held her breath and hid among the shadows of the hall. Matt was so close now, she could have touched him.

He stopped without warning.

His silhouette went rigid, except for the slow, wary turn of his head . . .

Away from her, in the opposite direction.

He listened. And waited. And finally passed her by.

She heard the sound of a door opening and closing. And then more brisk footsteps, fading at last into an eerie silence.

Lucy didn't stay to see if he'd come back.

As quietly as she could, she hurried to the main doors and slipped out into the snow.

The daylight she'd hoped to find was gone.

Dusk had already fallen, and deep drifts covered the street in front of the church.

Lucy wondered if the route to Irene's had been plowed. She hated the thought of being delayed on the roads—it was already going to take extra time just to wade around the block to the car. She didn't dare shortcut through the cemetery and run the risk of Matt seeing her.

What had Matt been doing in the old church anyway?

She couldn't help wondering what he'd been looking at so intently, why he'd seemed so upset. If she hadn't been such a coward, she could have examined the altar for herself. But she didn't have time to think about that now—there were more important things to worry about.

She felt frozen by the time she reached the car—even more frozen by the time she'd scraped all the ice off the back and side windows and windshield. A high snowbank had formed around the Corvette, and when Lucy realized she couldn't dig out, she climbed into the front seat, slammed the door, and let out a yell of frustration.

The clock on the dashboard read seven o'clock.

And the snow was still coming down.

I can't do this anymore.

Lucy leaned her head on the steering wheel.

I thought I could face everything alone. Fight everything . . . decide everything . . . solve everything. All on my own.

But I just can't.

She turned on the dome light in the ceiling. She pulled her purse from under the seat and found a crumpled business card in her wallet. After repeating the numbers printed there, she punched them in on her cell phone. And when the familiar voice finally answered, she breathed a deep sigh of relief.

"Dakota," Lucy said, "I need your help."

14

"Carbon monoxide," Dakota said solemnly.

Lucy stared at her, assuming an explanation would follow.

"Don't you know better than to sit in your car with the motor running?" Dakota frowned. "You could've died of carbon monoxide poisoning."

Lucy considered this. "Actually, that would have been the bright spot in my day."

"First, freezing. Now, carbon monoxide."

"I'm trying to be creative."

The two of them sat across from each other in the diner. The air was stuffy, thick with steam and old grease and cigarette smoke. After the dankness of the church cellar, Lucy breathed it in like perfume.

"I had my window cracked open," she defended herself.

"Not wide enough."

"Well . . . it's not exactly the best part of town to be stranded in."

"You fall asleep with some stranger whose entrails are hanging out, and you're worried about being mugged?"

"Ssh!"

"Sorry."

Their server arrived, setting plates of burgers and fries in front of them, sliding tall chocolate malteds across the tabletop. She slapped their bill down with an automatic smile, then walked back to a counter packed with customers.

Lucy took a bite of her extra-rare hamburger. A salad used to get her through the whole day, but lately she'd been craving more than just lettuce. In fact, she hadn't realized till now just how famished she was.

"I can't do this anymore," she announced, out loud this time, and around a huge mouthful of burger, pickle, and onion.

"Can't do what?" Dakota raised one eyebrow. "Eat?"

"No, not eat. I mean . . ."

"I know what you mean." Leaning forward, Dakota touched Lucy's hand. "I'm not making light of this. I'm just worried about you."

Lucy gave a vague nod. "Irene wants to put me away."

"Is that what she said?"

"Actually, I think she called it a 'nice long rest.' But she was serious, I could tell."

Dakota was philosophical. "It's a grown-up thing. My parents go through it about every three months—they threaten to lock us all up, and then they sort of forget about it."

"Dakota, what am I going to do?"

The two girls stared at each other.

"I don't know," Dakota said at last. "But thank you for telling me . . ."

Lucy *had* told her.

She'd waited in the car for Dakota to rescue her, and she'd argued with herself the whole time.

She'd given her word to Jared—just as she'd given her word to Katherine, just as she'd kept Byron's confidences. And maybe it *was* just coincidence that Katherine and Byron were both dead now—or maybe she really *was* bad luck—but if something happened to Dakota because of *her*, Lucy knew it would be the last straw. She'd never be able to forgive herself. She'd never be able to live with one more death on her conscience.

She'd heard the old truck wheezing around the corner, and even then she couldn't make up her mind. Dakota had brought shovels, and when the girls finally managed to excavate the Corvette, Lucy had suddenly thrown her arms around Dakota's neck.

"It's just a car," Dakota reminded her. "Not brain surgery."

"It's not about the car." Lucy was trying so hard to fight back tears, but she knew Dakota could hear her crying. "I've really got to talk to you."

"Is this the 'later where no one can hear us' thing you were trying to tell me this morning?"

"Yes. Where's a good place?"

Dakota thought a moment. "Your aunt's house. She's not there right now."

"How do you know?"

"Because I stopped by to see if you were okay. Come on—I'll follow you."

Dakota was right—Irene's house was deserted.

And when Lucy checked the answering machine, she heard Irene's voice announcing piles of paperwork to catch up on and very late hours at the office tonight. For once, Lucy was relieved to have the house all to herself. She fixed hot chocolate, then she and Dakota sat down at the kitchen table.

If you want to live . . . you mustn't tell anyone . . .

Katherine's warning still echoed in Lucy's ears. And though Lucy had kept that promise as best she could, even death seemed better now than carrying the burden alone.

"Dakota," Lucy announced, "this is going to take a while."

They'd spent the next three hours deep in conversation.

And Lucy had told her everything.

From that first night of fleeing into the cemetery, to Matt's strange behavior this evening at the church altar.

Everything.

At the beginning, Dakota kept quiet. A question here and there, a point that needed clarification—but generally, silence and a steady, solemn gaze. When Lucy finally exhausted herself and leaned back in the kitchen chair, only then did Dakota move, as though shaking off the spell of Lucy's narrative.

"Wow," she said quietly.

"Just 'wow'? That's it?"

"I don't know what else to say. I mean . . . you really expect me to believe all this?"

Lucy's heart sank. She gave a miserable nod.

"I do." Dakota nodded. "I *do* believe all this."

"You . . . do?"

"Lucy, I told you before. I believe in everything."

So simple. Just like that. Lucy hadn't known whether to laugh or to cry.

"But I'm cold inside," Dakota added. "I'll have to keep thinking about this. It's a lot to take in all at once."

"Imagine how I feel," Lucy replied glumly.

"I don't think I can. I think that part would be totally beyond my range of comprehension."

Lucy managed a smile. But one nagging question had kept at her, looming larger than all the others.

"Do you really think he's Byron's brother?" she asked.

"Well . . . why would he make up something like that?"

"I don't know, that's what bothers me so much. I mean . . . why would he suddenly show up now? Asking all those questions about Byron's funeral?"

"There could be a million reasons. Just because Byron never talked about him doesn't mean they're not brothers. And if he *looks* that much like Byron—"

"He does. So much, it's actually scary."

"And didn't you say Father Matt was trying to find some of Byron's relatives?"

"To help with his grandmother, yes."

"Then I'd say Jared is the least of your problems," Dakota concluded. "Considering everything you've told me, and putting it all in perspective."

Lost in their own thoughts, the girls sat for a while, neither of them speaking. It had been Lucy who finally broke the silence.

"Dakota . . . why *me?*"

"Why *not* you?" Dakota's answer was quick, but not unkind. "Remember that night in the bookstore when you saw Byron at the window?"

How could Lucy forget it? Uncomfortably, she lowered her eyes.

"Do you remember what I told you?" Dakota persisted. "About your being gifted? And brave?"

"Sort of."

"And how I knew you had an aura—a very special energy—like Byron's, only a whole lot stronger?"

"I remember."

"And how I told you to trust your instincts?"

Lucy nodded.

"So . . . what are your instincts telling you now?"

Lucy looked up into Dakota's calm stare. She wrapped her fingers tightly around her cup, but her hot chocolate had gone cold.

"I don't know," she admitted. "I don't feel like I know *anything* anymore. Nothing makes sense."

"But don't you see—that's just it. Things *never* make sense till they're *supposed* to. Answers don't come till we're able to understand them. And truths can't be revealed till we're ready to accept what they are."

A slight frown touched Dakota's brow. Her voice grew pensive as she reached over to squeeze Lucy's hand.

"This is one thing I believe. I believe we don't discover our purpose all at once. I believe we have to be eased into it, little by little . . . sort of like practicing. Till we're strong enough to handle it on our own."

"So . . . you're saying . . . what exactly are you saying?"

Lucy had wanted explanations. An end to all the madness. But what she'd gotten instead was Dakota's quiet prophecy.

"You've been chosen for something. Some destiny that's way beyond anything we could ever imagine."

"Don't tell me that, Dakota. Just tell me what to do!"

"I can't. But when it's time . . . you'll know."

So now they were sitting here eating at the run-down diner.

Because after their conversation, Lucy had needed noise and life and a sense of normalcy, no matter how false it might turn out to be.

She dragged one French fry through a thick pool of ketchup.

The red liquid reminded her of blood, and how she'd had to shower and change again before they'd come here, to wash away the stains and the smell and the shock of her day. From a distance she heard Dakota talking to her, and her mind snapped back into the present.

"What did you say?" Lucy asked.

"I said, you need to write everything down."

"Write what down?"

"Everything. Everything you told me. Everything that's happened to you since you came to Pine Ridge."

Lucy made a face. "What good would that do?"

"Well, just think about it. If you died mysteriously or disappeared again, you'd have documentation."

"That's a pleasant thought."

"You should keep a record of every experience. Like a diary."

"Are you planning to publish my memoirs after I die and make a lot of money?"

"No. I'm being practical." Dakota sucked

thoughtfully on her straw. "So . . . when are you going back?"

"To the church?" Lucy gave a weary shrug. "I can't just leave him there. But it'll be harder to get inside this time—and I *really* don't want to get arrested for breaking and entering."

"Maybe I can help."

"If you come with me, he'll know I told."

"But if he looks at my face, he'll know I'm very trustworthy."

Lucy couldn't help but smile. "You have a point."

"I just can't believe you didn't take toilet paper."

"What?"

"You brought all that other stuff for him, but you didn't bring toilet paper."

Lucy stared at Dakota. Dakota stared back.

"No toilet paper," Dakota sounded distressed. "And even worse . . . where's he supposed to go to the bathroom?"

"You know, I really don't think—" Lucy began, but before she could finish, a young man with spiked orange hair raced up to their booth and immediately plopped down beside Dakota.

Dakota just as immediately looked annoyed. "Lucy, this is my brother, Texas."

"Texas Montana?" The words were out before she could stop them, but Lucy managed a quick recovery. "The musician, right? Nice to meet you."

"Hey, how ya doin'?" The guy jerked his chin at her, though his attention was focused on Dakota. "You heard the latest?"

Dakota deliberately mulled this over. "The latest. Meaning . . . some earth-shattering event that actually broke up band practice tonight?"

"Couldn't practice without my bass guitarist, right?" he threw back at her. "Greg got called in."

"Greg works for the sheriff's department," Dakota explained.

Lucy nodded politely, but a prickle of apprehension was starting up her spine. Dakota's brother was so wound up, he was almost shaking.

"So he knows about that murder, right?" Texas went on. "That Wanda Carver girl?"

Lucy put her hands on the edge of the table. Her knuckles went white as she began to squeeze.

"You won't believe what happened to her." Texas's face was incredulous. "I mean—this is so, like, right out of the movies!"

"She fell," Lucy insisted firmly. "Someone pushed her."

"Yeah, well, maybe, but that's not all. And you can't say anything, 'cause the cops don't want anybody to know."

He motioned both girls closer. They leaned in over the table. He placed one arm over each of their shoulders and ducked his head down between them.

"That girl was drained, man," he whispered. "There was hardly any blood left in her whole body."

15

Lucy stared up at the bedroom ceiling.

She was holding the medallion Matt had given her, stroking it absently with her fingers. *"Someone gave me this a long time ago . . . an ancient holy symbol . . . helped through some pretty rough times . . . give it a try . . . special to you . . ."*

She'd almost forgotten about it through the drama of these last few days. She'd stashed it in her nightstand, where it had slipped to the back and gotten wedged behind the drawer. But tonight, after she'd washed Jared's clothes, and rounded up more towels and blankets, and fallen exhausted into bed, she'd found the medallion again, and she'd remembered Matt's words, and she'd longed to be comforted.

She still couldn't make out the medallion's design. Nor had she been able to discover what the carved symbol meant. The one time she'd tried to ask Matt about it, they'd been interrupted.

But now she squeezed it tightly with both hands. She'd been lying here for hours, unable to sleep and unable to turn off her thoughts.

"There was hardly any blood left in her whole body."

The death of Wanda Carver haunted her. The last moments of Wanda's life and what the poor girl must have gone through—the panic, the absolute terror and pain . . .

"The cops don't want anybody to know . . ."

And Lucy hadn't known either.

That day when she'd bumped into the cheerleaders, when she'd had that first inkling of Wanda's death . . .

How could she have known then that the death she'd seen in her vision would turn out to be a murder?

"I tried to warn her," Lucy whispered. "I tried to help."

And what was it Byron had told her? That day they'd been together, an eternity ago?

"You'll try to warn people, but they won't believe you . . . You'll try to save people, but you'll fail."

Lucy tossed restlessly beneath the covers.

It didn't surprise her that the police would be close-mouthed about Wanda's death. For a thorough investigation, they'd need to keep certain clues confidential. And they'd definitely want to prevent an outbreak of hysteria in the community. But who—*what*—could have done something this brutal to another human being? It *couldn't* be human itself, Lucy rationalized—it would have to be some sort of wild animal . . .

An animal that could blend into shadows . . .

That could stalk someone undetected . . .

That could rip a man's body to shreds with one bite . . .

A sinister chill crept through her. She huddled beneath the blankets, like a child afraid of the dark.

She was letting her imagination take over. Even an animal wouldn't be able to do what had been done to Wanda Carver. Even an animal couldn't drain a body of that much blood.

But what if it could?

What if there really *were* some animal that could do those things?

She was afraid to look at the curtains now, or

the sliding glass door . . . afraid to peer out on the balcony. Suddenly she was afraid to look anywhere, afraid even to move.

Because what if some horrible evil *had* come to Pine Ridge?

Hiding in cemeteries . . . roaming through woods . . . watching through windows in the night?

And what if I've seen it?

Her heart was pumping out of control, ice-cold terror coursing through her veins. The whole room was closing in.

And what if I've heard it?

For suddenly she sensed that she *had*. At some long-ago time, in some long-forgotten dream, she'd looked into its face and heard the sound of its voice . . .

And it touched me.

Like something was touching her now . . .

For one brief instant, the memory burned fierce and deep, and Lucy almost remembered.

Almost . . . but not quite.

Groggily, she sat up and reached for the blankets.

They were folded around her ankles, though

she didn't recall turning them down. The medallion had dropped to the floor.

I must have dozed off.

She tucked the covers under her chin.

Almost . . . she could almost remember . . .

That face, that voice, that touch . . .

So dear to her . . .

And so deadly.

16

The change in Lucy would be slow.

A transformation so subtle she would scarcely even recognize it in herself.

A delicate altering of the senses . . . a slight shifting of perceptions . . . so gradual . . . so very gradual . . .

Leaving emptiness in place of memories.

And realities where only disbelief had been before.

But most of all . . . most important of all . . . fixing *him* first and foremost in her mind.

It was *already* happening, in fact.

He had watched from the balcony tonight— watched her deep distress and restlessness—and he had suspected that she was trying to remember him.

Yes, Lucy, you need to remember. The one connected

*to you now . . . the only one who can fill that ache
inside you . . .*

And when she fell asleep those few brief
seconds, he had crept in to her. Gently turned
down her blankets. Caressed her with a slow
and tender touch.

Yes, Lucy, that's right. Remember . . .

*Remember the way I lured you at the festival . . .
blindfolded you behind the tent . . . when I first
sucked the blood from your lip . . .*

Such a sweet addiction that had been. Reeling
him nearly senseless, with a craving he could
scarcely control . . .

But now his own blood flowed through her
veins.

His own blood, easing her through the
transition.

Ah yes . . . the transition . . .

For a sudden moment he forgot about Lucy.
Something like sadness swelled in his heart as
his thoughts searched through the past.

He closed his eyes and tried, himself, to
remember.

Tried to remember that first and wondrous
change.

But his thoughts remained dark. Dark thoughts of pain and death and begging and tears.

For him it'd been a long, long time. *Too long.*

And that sacred memory he'd sworn never to forget had been washed away by an eternity of bloodshed.

No! He would *not* think of it—he would *never* think of it!

He would think of Lucy instead. He would think of how she'd come to him just a few nights ago, pulled by something she couldn't see, longing for something she couldn't understand and wasn't sure she'd find.

He would think of how he'd been waiting for her as she'd stepped from the house. How he'd watched as she'd opened herself to all the secrets of the night.

For one brief moment she'd come to him.

Come to him and surrendered.

Wearing moonlight like a bridal gown, hair shimmering over bare shoulders, reaching for him, reaching, so full of hope, of life, while he'd started toward her, closer and closer, ready to take her, in fact . . . when the woman had appeared.

The woman—the aunt.

The one who made Lucy so sad.

Soon, Lucy . . . soon. You won't be sad anymore . . .

Tonight he'd bent over her pillow.

Smoothed her brow, and gently stroked her hair.

His lips had found the pulse at her throat . . . he'd smiled as she moaned in her dreams.

He'd watched her first few drowsy moments of fading sleep . . .

He'd felt the warm surrender in her body as he'd kissed her.

Yes . . .

Her dependence on him was growing, just as he'd planned.

Touch by touch . . . and lie by cunning lie.

17

"I should have known this would happen." Lucy yanked open the door to her locker and jerked out a stack of books. "I mean, I *figured* it would happen; I just didn't think it would be this *bad*."

Her first clue had been in homeroom. The whole class fell silent the second she walked in, and the few students bold enough to look at her seemed either extremely nervous or downright hostile.

"It's like I'm a witch or something," Lucy grumbled. "Like I should wear a big red letter on my shirt. *D* for doom, maybe. Or *BL* for bad luck."

"Or *BO* for back off," Dakota added helpfully. "Except then people might just think you smell bad." She stood directly behind Lucy, as though to shield her friend from the rush of students through the hall. "Everyone's paranoid, Lucy. Just ignore them."

"Ignore them? If they thought they could get away with it, they'd stampede right now and pulverize me into the floor."

"But they *wouldn't* get away with it." Dakota made a subtle gesture toward the office, where several police officers stood talking to Principal Howser. "Not with all the uniforms around."

"Right. Like *they'd* protect me."

The two of them shouldered their way to the vending machines. Dakota opted for trail mix, while Lucy, after some hesitation, finally chose a packet of beef jerky.

"What's that about?" Dakota nodded at the strip of dried meat as Lucy unwrapped it. "You always get potato chips."

"I don't know. Maybe I'm just craving protein today."

Choosing a table just inside the cafeteria door, they unloaded their books and sat down.

"So what about Jared?" Dakota lowered her voice, glancing around as if spies might pop out of the trash cans.

Lucy's tone clearly conveyed her distress. "I

couldn't get over there this morning. Irene was in a terrible mood, and I thought she was going to give me the third degree about missing school yesterday. But she didn't. She never even mentioned it."

Dakota shrugged. "That's good."

"And at the last minute I couldn't get the car to start. So she had to give me a ride."

"No problem. We can go after school."

"*If* we can sneak in," Lucy reminded her. She hesitated, then said, "So you haven't changed your mind since last night?"

"About what?"

"About believing me. You said you still had to think about things."

"I *am* still thinking about things. I'm *always* thinking about things. That has nothing to do with believing you." Dakota carefully examined several raisins that she'd pulled from the bag. "Of course I believe you. These look like dead flies—you don't think they are, do you?"

After a cursory glance, Lucy shook her head. "Have you heard any more about the murder?"

"Not much. But I think that *thing* we're not supposed to tell anyone is starting to get around.

You can't keep news like that secret for very long. People are acting really, really nervous."

"Is that why we're having an assembly this afternoon?"

"Probably. The police and the sheriff's department are both going to be there. I'm sure they'll tell us to be careful and to travel in groups. Maybe even impose a curfew for a while. And I've heard the Holiday Treasure Hunt might be canceled."

Dakota finished her snack. She crumpled the cellophane and slowly licked the tip of each finger.

"It's weird, isn't it?" Her gaze shifted toward the noisy, crowded hallway. "I didn't even know Wanda that well—I didn't even *like* her that much—but now that she's dead . . ." Her voice trailed off. She looked at Lucy with a troubled frown.

"What is it?" Lucy asked softly.

"Can you feel her missing? Can you feel an empty spot where she used to be?"

Lucy thought a long moment. "I felt it with Byron."

"Me, too. Even though you know death isn't

an end to things . . . or an end to life . . . or whatever. Still, when someone leaves this dimension, there's this hole left in their place. And the world seems to shift a little off balance, till that hole fills up again."

The girls lapsed into silence. It was Lucy who finally spoke.

"Do you know when Wanda's funeral is?"

"They haven't released her body yet." Dakota sounded sad. "I think the police are making an attempt to avoid a major panic. Her family's just devastated. Mr. Carver had a heart attack last night and ended up in the emergency room."

"Is he okay?"

Dakota nodded, twirling a strand of red hair. "I hope so. They want to watch him for a few days."

"This is so awful," Lucy murmured. "I mean, what do the police think really happened? Do they have any clues? Any suspects?"

"Well, first they'll say it was someone just passing through town. That nobody in Pine Ridge could have done such a horrible thing. Then I'd be willing to bet they'll target the university—check out all the weirdos there."

"What do *you* think?"

Dakota fixed her with a level gaze. "What do *you* think?"

"I didn't see who killed her." Lucy sighed. "I didn't even see her actually dying, much less being murdered. God . . . I wish now that I had."

"Be careful what you wish for," Dakota said solemnly.

As the girls hurried to class, Lucy was struck by an oppressive air of mourning everywhere she looked. The shrines, the flowers and special presents, the whispers and tear-swollen eyes. It seemed that Pine Ridge High would never be allowed to recover from one tragedy before being hit by another.

Just like me, Lucy thought.

She and Dakota slipped into their seats just as roll was being taken. When Lucy heard her own name called, she answered but kept her eyes on her desk. It wasn't just wariness and anger she was sensing now from the other kids around her—it was fear.

The sudden realization surprised her. She could feel it in the air, sizzling like electricity—

suspicion and distrust coming at her from every direction. When the intercom came on, asking her to report to the office, she was almost relieved. She shrugged at Dakota, who threw her a questioning look. And as she neared the administration desk, she found someone unexpected waiting for her.

"Lucy." Matt greeted her with a smile. "Great. I wasn't sure you were even here today."

He thanked one of the secretaries, then ushered Lucy out into the hall.

"Come on," he joked. "Let's talk in my confessional."

"You mean I'm in some kind of trouble?"

"What possible kind of trouble could *you* be in?"

"Well, I didn't kill Wanda Carver, if that's what you're thinking."

Matt gave her that "get serious" look he was so good at. He seemed perfectly normal today, his usual self, not at all like he'd been at the church last night. Maybe he'd been dealing with a personal problem, Lucy decided. Even priests had problems, didn't they? She felt guilty now for spying on him.

Matt led her into his tiny office, shut the door, and motioned for her to sit down.

"Oh, I see you're wearing the medallion."

Lucy flushed. How could he tell? When she'd put it on this morning, she'd slid it down the front of her blouse. Only one small section of the chain showed—the part hanging just above her breasts—the rest of it was covered by her collar and long hair.

Self-consciously, she adjusted it around her throat. "I really like it. But you still haven't told me—"

"Where it's from? Hmmm . . . somewhere in Europe, I think. Now—anything you want to tell *me?*"

Lucy couldn't decide if he was kidding or not. "Should there be?" she asked cautiously.

"It's just that I covered for you yesterday when you skipped school."

"*You* did?"

"Yes. I committed a small sin on your behalf." Matt sighed. "I told Mr. Howser you were helping me out with a very important project. Important enough to keep you out of your classes the entire day."

"But . . . why?"

"Because Dakota said you had an important reason for being gone, and that was good enough for me." He lifted an eyebrow, his expression deadpan. "So . . . what? I *shouldn't* have believed her?"

"It's. . . it's not that . . ."

"Don't worry. She didn't tell me what the reason was, and I didn't ask."

"I . . . well . . . thanks."

"You're welcome. And I'm not trying to pry into your business. But if this reason of yours has anything to do with—"

"There's something I need you to see," Lucy said quickly. She wasn't exactly sure why she'd thought of the special-delivery headstone at that precise second. But since she'd planned on telling him anyway, now seemed as opportune a time as any. Besides, what better way to divert Matt's attention from the tricky matter at hand?

"You need *me* to see?" Matt echoed, surprised.

"Yes. It happened again."

"What did?"

"You remember the night you came over, and

I told you about that blanket and Byron's jacket in the car?"

Matt was beginning to look dubious. "Yes . . ."

"Well, something else happened. Something even worse this time. I got a delivery—"

"Delivery?" He picked up a mug from the desk and began stirring the contents with a spoon.

"A special delivery." Lucy explained. "In an unmarked truck. The box was addressed to me, and when I opened it, I found . . ."

She'd really thought she could recount the incident without emotion. Yet now the initial horror swept over her again, leaving her voice slightly unsteady.

"It was a headstone. And it had letters carved on it. R I P Angela Foster."

Matt didn't take his eyes off her. He set the mug back on the desk, his face pensive.

"You . . . you actually *saw* this headstone?" he asked.

"Of course I saw it. I opened the box. I totally panicked, and then I dumped it off the porch."

"You . . ."

"Dumped it off the porch. Into the bushes where no one could see it. I didn't want Irene

146

finding it. That would have been too cruel."

Matt sat down. "And this happened . . . when?"

"Two nights ago," Lucy admitted reluctantly. "The night of Angela's vigil."

"And you're just mentioning it *now*?"

"I didn't know what else to do!"

"Well, if this is some kids' idea of a joke, maybe it's time for me to get involved."

"And what if it's not a joke?"

"Then the police should definitely be notified. For God's sake, why didn't you call them?"

"I wanted to. At first I thought if they saw it, then they'd finally have to believe me about all the other stuff I've told them. But . . . if you won't even believe me . . ."

"Hey, have I said anything about not believing you?"

"And now . . . with this murder . . . and Sheriff Stark asking me questions . . . and the way everyone's looking at me—"

"You were afraid," Matt concluded quietly. "Of course you were. No wonder you wanted to keep your distance from school."

"I still think someone's trying to send me a message. A warning."

"I don't know *what* to think about all this. If it's a prank, then Principal Howser should know about it. But if it turns out to be a real piece of evidence? You *have* to tell the police, Lucy—it could be crucial to finding Angela."

"Can't *you* just tell them you found it somewhere?"

"Wonderful. Now you want me to lie again."

"Matt, I'm confiding in you. If you tell, you'll be breaking your vows."

"Is there a name for this, besides blackmail?" Shaking his head in defeat, Matt began shuffling through some scattered papers on the desk. "Let me have a look at the headstone first. Then we can decide what to do."

Lucy didn't answer. Matt stopped arranging papers and focused on her dejected face.

"Lucy, like I said before, I don't mean to pry into your private life. But if you can't face coming to school . . . and especially now with the police hanging around . . ."

A long pause followed. Matt's face softened along with his voice.

"The thing is, I've heard all the rumors about what you told Wanda Carver. And of course, I think it's all bull—nonsense. And just so you know, I've had my *own* conversation with Sheriff Stark about your credibility. I think he and I are clear on the subject."

"You mean, you talked to him and took my side?"

"Great." A smile played at the corners of his mouth. "Now you're implying I'm not a good enough reference."

He got up and walked to the front of his desk, then casually leaned back against it. He seemed to be in deep thought, his eyes focused above her on the wall, his fingers running absentmindedly along his collar. The innocent gesture was almost seductive, and Lucy couldn't stop watching him. Embarrassed, she felt another hot flush creep over her cheeks.

What is wrong *with you?*

Dakota was right—no wonder the whole female population of Pine Ridge High was in love with Matt. While he, on the other hand, was completely clueless.

"The sheriff told me you'd had a dream." Matt shifted his gaze back to her. "And that you were trying to help."

Lucy wished they didn't have to talk about this. She could feel guilt and depression tightening around her like a straitjacket.

"I did want to help," she agreed. "But I never thought it would turn into anything like this."

"And this dream," Matt continued quietly. "Do you have a lot of dreams like that?"

She hesitated a second. She chose her words with care. "You mean nightmares? I have them all the time."

"I meant dreams that tend to come true . . . in one way or another."

"I just . . . have dreams. They don't necessarily come true or mean anything at all. They're . . . you know . . . just dreams."

Matt's fingers slid from his collar to his face. Lightly he stroked his chin.

"Does Dr. Fielding still have you on medication?"

"Yes." Lucy shifted uncomfortably. Why was everyone so interested in her dreams all of a sudden? Why was *Matt*? "Sometimes the medicine gives me weird dreams. The doctor says that's normal."

Matt stared at her without speaking. Looked

into her eyes for several long moments, then finally nodded.

"Well." His shrug was philosophical. "Who can tell about dreams anyway? Sometimes they make sense; most of the time they don't."

"I did run into her once. Wanda Carver." *Now why did I say that?* "Literally. Going through a door."

"Well, there you are. Not so hard to figure out why she ended up in one of your dreams after all."

"I wish you'd convince the school of that."

Matt flashed that teasing smile. "Don't worry. I won't let them burn you at the stake." Reaching over, he ruffled her hair. "Now. Let's talk about another motive I had for bringing you here."

"What's that?"

"Don't sound so suspicious. It's good news."

"There *is* such a thing?"

He laughed at that. He folded his arms across his chest and stretched one long leg over the other.

"First," he announced dramatically, "I spoke with Mrs. Wetherly about your staying there."

This was definitely something Lucy hadn't expected. She sat up with a hopeful smile. "And?"

"She liked the idea very much. I told her about your aunt being away for a while. And that you needed a job and a place to stay. And that you could do light housework. And that you'd make a very good companion." Again that deadpan look. "Much better than a pet, in fact."

For the first time in days, Lucy brightened. "Really? She'll give me a chance?"

"By all means."

"That's so great! Now all I have to do is convince Aunt Irene."

"Piece of cake," Matt assured her. "How about I give her a call and see if she'll let me drop by this evening? I'm guessing you'd rather be gone when I ask her?"

"I'd be too nervous to hang around for that. But if you could get there before she comes home, then I can show you the headstone."

"Good idea."

"Do you think she'll say yes?"

"When it comes to the art of persuasion, being a priest has definite advantages."

"Thank you!" Before she even knew what she was doing, Lucy was on her feet, hugging him tightly. "Thank you so much—you don't know what this means to me—"

Abruptly she broke off.

Matt had already reached for her hands, to untangle himself from her hug. And now, as Lucy glanced up at him, she could see that his face was practically touching hers.

He was smiling, and his deep blue gaze seemed to draw her in. And for one instant, it was easy to imagine him stripped of his vows, with the tenderness of long-ago kisses still lingering upon his lips.

Flustered, Lucy tried to step back, but his arms were in the way.

"Thank you, Matt," she mumbled. "It seems like you're always there to rescue me."

Matt was the first to break eye contact. As the laughter slowly began to fade from his smile, something almost poignant took its place . . . and then was gone.

"Well, isn't that what priests are supposed to do?" He gave her a brief, brotherly pat on the shoulder. "At least, I think it mentions that somewhere in the Official How-to-Be-a-Priest Handbook."

And then he was behind his desk again, and Lucy was standing by the door, trying to look anywhere but at him.

"Now," Matt said brusquely. "I have more good news."

Curious, she watched him open the window blinds wider. Then he checked his appointment calendar and distractedly adjusted the collar at his neck.

"It's news I've been hoping for," he added.

"And what's that?"

"Byron Wetherly has a brother."

18

"A . . . brother?"

Lucy wondered if her voice sounded as stunned as she felt. She quickly sank down into the chair.

"I got a letter yesterday," Matt announced as he sat back down. "To tell you the truth, I didn't really expect to hear anything so fast. I thought it'd take months, at least."

"Byron's brother sent you a letter?"

"Well, you know how I was hoping there might be another relative somewhere— someone who could take care of Mrs. Wetherly?" Matt looked pleased with himself. "Sometimes this clergy connection can be a wonderful thing. It's amazing what the church can dig up."

"I don't understand."

"All I did was put the word out. I figured since the family's Catholic, that'd be an easy place to start. And it's not like their name's all that common."

Lucy shook her head. She sat stiff in her chair.

"My idea worked." Matt grinned. "Like a charm, in fact."

"So . . . what about this letter?"

"It's quite a story."

"I bet."

"Either one hell of a miracle, or one hell of a coincidence," he added. "Take your pick."

Before Lucy could answer, he leaned back in his chair, folded his arms behind his head, and began to explain.

"Apparently, Byron's father abandoned the family years ago, when the kids were small. But for some reason, he ended up taking this one son away with him. They moved out of the country, there was never any correspondence between the parents after that, so this boy never had a clue about his former life."

Matt paused. His eyes strayed to the window, to the snowy world beyond, and his expression grew troubled.

"It seems the father is—was—very wealthy. The boy spent most of his life in boarding schools."

"That's sad," Lucy murmured.

"I know. Taking a kid away from his own family, then never spending any time with him. What's the point?"

"So how old is he?"

"He didn't say. The tone of the letter sounds older though . . . you know, mature."

"Where did they live?"

"Different places. Europe, mostly."

"What's his name?"

"Jared. Jared Wetherly."

So it *was* true. The mysterious stranger she'd befriended *had* been telling the truth—even though he still had a lot of explaining to do.

Lucy felt almost dizzy with relief. She twisted her hands together in her lap and kept her gaze on Matt.

"But now," Matt went on solemnly, "it turns out the father's been sick for a long time. The son didn't know about it. *Nobody* knew about it. One day Jared called home, and his father's dying. And *that's* when his father finally told him the whole story."

"So . . . Jared didn't remember anything at all about his childhood?"

"No. But his father *did* mention Pine Ridge—that was the last place the family'd been together."

"Did he . . . say anything about a house fire?"

Matt winced. "I heard those stories, too, about Byron's mother."

"Do you think they're true? Do you think she's really in an institution somewhere?"

"I don't know. I'm not sure anybody really knows. But I'm not gonna be the one to bring it up."

Matt rose from his chair. Once more he stood beside the windowpane, his silhouette etched blackly against the pristine backdrop of snow.

"How would you feel?" he murmured. "Suddenly finding out you had a life . . . a past . . . a whole history you never even knew you had?"

Lucy's thoughts flashed wildly to the cellar. What awful thing could have happened to Jared before he'd even had a chance to phone Matt? And what if Jared had *died*? What if he'd had all those hopes . . . come all this way . . . and then died before reconnecting with his family?

With an effort, she picked up the conversation again.

"So . . . what else did he say in the letter?"

"He didn't know he had a grandmother, of course. He seemed really happy about it . . . but scared, too. He said he'd come here as soon as he could."

"Now?" Lucy asked quickly. "This week?"

Matt shrugged. "I don't know. I offered to meet him *when* he wanted, *where* he wanted— but he said there were things he needed to take care of now that his father was dead. He couldn't be exactly sure when he'd be here. So he said he'd just contact me once he got to town."

"That's . . . great. So he could actually be on his way here right now."

"Or not."

"Or he could already *be* here, maybe." Lucy tried her best to sound casual. "You know . . . working up his courage."

"Maybe . . . but I doubt it."

Clasping his hands behind his back, Matt began to pace. Slow, measured steps from the door to the window and back again.

"It's funny how things work out, though," he mused. "Jared finding all this out from his father right when we needed him to. I mean, when you look at situations like this, and how perfectly they fit together, you can't *doubt* there's a Power out there. Someone—some divine Force—whatever you choose to call it— in total control. Keeping things synchronized and running on time, just like clockwork. Just the way they're supposed to."

Lucy didn't comment. She was in no mood for divine philosophies at the moment.

"So," she asked him, "are you sure you still want me to stay with Mrs. Wetherly? Since she'll have her grandson here now?"

"Of course; you have to stay! They'll be strangers to each other."

"Well . . . I'm a stranger, too."

"No, you're not. Not like that." Matt spread his hands in appeal. "I think it's really important for you to be there when they meet. And besides—we don't want Mrs. Dempsey to be the first impression Jared has of Pine Ridge."

"Hmmm. Good point."

"Jared needs to get *acquainted* with his

160

grandmother first, not play nursemaid. And we don't even know how long he'll stay."

"You mean, you don't think he'll move here?"

"Would *you*, if you had all the money in the world?"

Lucy became instantly alarmed. "But he won't put her in a nursing home, will he?"

"I don't know why he would."

"Because of what you said—because he has money. Maybe he'll think she's a burden. Maybe he'll sell her house and stick her in one of those awful places. I thought we were trying to save her—not make things worse!"

"Wait—slow down—"

"Maybe he shouldn't come here at all! What if he totally ruins her life?"

"Whoa—*whoa!* Since when is everyone such a potential villain?" Looking amused now, Matt tried to calm her down. "Give him a chance, okay? I mean, if he *doesn't* want to take care of her, then he can use all that money to hire round-the-clock nurses."

"Matt, promise me—"

"Yes, yes, I *promise*. I *won't* let him put her in a nursing home."

But Lucy was only mildly pacified. "I don't want her hurt."

"I don't either. Which is why I'm glad you're gonna be there with her. To keep an eye on things."

Lucy pondered this a moment. Finally she gave a reluctant nod. "So when are you going to tell her?"

"I haven't quite figured that out yet."

"What do you mean? You have to tell her before Jared *gets* here." *Which means* now—*since he's hiding in the church cellar right this minute.*

Matt slid his hands into his pockets. He'd stopped pacing now, but his eyes were still angled toward the floor.

"The thing is," he said carefully, "Jared asked me to wait. I think he's still trying to get used to the idea himself. And since he's not exactly sure when he can get to town . . ."

"You can't just spring it on her."

"I know. But we shouldn't let her worry about it ahead of time either." Matt's voice went low and solemn. "With her stroke and all, and Byron's dying . . ."

And Katherine, too, Lucy thought sadly, *and so*

many other things that you and I will probably never even know about . . .

"Matt, what are you trying to say?"

"That we have to be careful. Because another big shock could kill her."

19

"I can guarantee you, Father Matt won't be at the old church anytime this afternoon," Dakota said.

Lucy held her hands out toward the vents. After making a quick pass through the grocery store, she and Dakota had been sitting in the parking lot for nearly fifteen minutes, waiting for the truck to warm up. The heater was straining, but spurting out only tepid air at best. Irritated, Dakota reached over, slammed the heels of both hands against the dashboard, then leaned back with a satisfied smile as a rush of hot air blasted over them.

"It's all in the touch," she said modestly when Lucy flashed her a grateful smile.

"So how do you know Matt—Father Matt—won't be there?"

"You heard what he said at our assembly

about being glad to stay after school if anyone still needed counseling. Didn't you see that stampede to the sign-up sheet? He might as well bring his pajamas and toothbrush, and camp out in his office indefinitely."

The two were silent a long moment.

Finally Dakota asked, "Do you think he *wears* pajamas?"

"Another esoteric mystery of the church," Lucy teased, trying not to blush. Just that brief, accidental encounter in Matt's office, and suddenly she could feel every detail of his body pressed to hers. *Well, that's one situation I might never tell Dakota about.*

Annoyed with herself, she turned to the window and leaned her cheek against the frosty glass.

"I bet he doesn't," Dakota reflected. "I bet he doesn't even wear underwear. I bet he sleeps naked."

"Dakota!"

"Well, I don't know, do you? But even if there's some rule priests have to follow—like, they *have* to sleep in black pajamas, or a black nightshirt, or black underwear—he just doesn't seem the type to go along with the crowd."

"Why don't you just ask him?"

"Maybe I will. He's helping out at the soup kitchen in the morning. Maybe I'll ask him then."

"Good idea. I'll come and help, too.

"And then when we're dishing out oatmeal together, and he wants to know if there's anything bothering me that I'd like to talk about, I'll just say, Father Matt, the thing that's bothering me most of all is wondering what you wear in bed."

"I bet Mrs. Dempsey would know." Amused, Lucy turned to face Dakota. "She's the housekeeper at the rectory, right?—she probably knows *all* their secrets."

"Especially Father Paul's."

"Why Father Paul's?"

"She's been in love with him for the last forty years. Everybody knows that."

"Mrs. Dempsey and Father Paul?"

"I know," Dakota made a face. "Not something you'd even *remotely* care to imagine."

Both girls burst out laughing. They laughed and laughed, from the grocery store till the truck finally rattled to a stop behind the cemetery.

"Oh, I hurt," Lucy moaned, holding her stomach.

Dakota slumped over the steering wheel and drew a deep breath. "Me, too."

"I can't remember when I've laughed this hard."

"Me neither."

"Especially when I shouldn't be laughing at all."

The laughter died. Dakota fixed Lucy with a sympathetic stare. "Life is extremely weird right now. *Your* life in particular. If this isn't the perfect time for you to laugh, I don't know what is."

But Lucy didn't answer right away. She stared down at the floor until Dakota reached over and took her hand.

"Thanks for telling me about your meeting with Father Matt," Dakota said. "Didn't his news about Jared make you feel a lot better?"

"Not particularly."

"The main thing is, you know now that Jared really *is* Byron's brother. And maybe if the two of you put your heads together, you can start figuring out some of this stuff."

"He didn't even know Byron." Lucy sighed. "What good is that going to do?"

"But he might have all these buried memories . . . things he hasn't thought about in years. Maybe by talking you'll find some new pieces of the puzzle. Whatever it is."

"I suppose," Lucy murmured.

"I mean . . . I've *heard* of people healing themselves." Releasing Lucy's hand, Dakota shifted and leaned against the door. "It might not be that common, but it's not impossible either. Some people have such powerful thoughts—such focused minds—they can actually make things move. They can bend objects and even levitate. Shamans . . . medicine men . . . some of those Bible guys . . . What you saw with Jared doesn't have to be a bad thing, you know. Sometimes what seems like magic can really be a gift."

"You mean . . . like *me*. Like the visions."

Dakota's shrug was noncommittal. "You know what's weird, though?"

"Besides everything?"

"When you touched Jared and had those visions, you didn't get really sick afterward."

"You're right." The car was almost *too* hot now, yet Lucy shivered. "I never thought of that."

"Remember that day you ran into Wanda? And then you had to go to the infirmary? And the other visions you told me about—it was almost like you had seizures?"

"So . . . what's your point?"

"I don't have a point. I just thought it was weird."

"Okay. That's one more mystery I'll add to my list."

"Maybe it's the quality time."

"Excuse me?"

"Quality time. Bonding time. You . . . you . . ." Dakota was searching for words. "You *helped* him . . . you *nurtured* him. You were kind. You made him feel safe. You gained his trust."

"You make him sound like a stray animal or something."

"Well," Dakota said seriously, "every living creature needs compassion, doesn't it?"

Lucy stared at her friend, at the depth of conviction in Dakota's eyes.

"Yes, Dakota, you're right. Even if we can't

always understand, we can at least show some compassion."

She pulled away, then glanced anxiously out the windshield. After yesterday's big snow, the cemetery looked like a vast white ocean, with softly curling waves where headstones used to be. The Wetherly mausoleum stood apart and alone, as if shunned by the rest of the dead.

"I wish you didn't have to sneak in the back way," Dakota said softly.

"Someone might see me at the front."

"They'll see your footprints anyway if they come around the side of the building. And you don't even know if you can get in like you did before. Then what?"

"Then I'll have to think of something else."

"I'll wait for you right here."

"But I don't know how long I'll be. Are you sure you don't want to leave for a while? Come back in an hour or so?"

"Okay, I'll get some coffee. And *then* I'll wait right here."

Stuffing her backpack full of groceries, Lucy started to open her door, then turned back to Dakota.

"What if Jared's not there? What if he turns out to be like the warning in my notebook? And like Byron outside the bookshop window?"

"He'll be there," Dakota insisted. "Things are all starting to make sense for a change, Lucy. He mailed that letter. He came here to Pine Ridge, but something happened to him before he had a chance to call Father Matt. The thing we don't know is . . . what attacked him?"

"The same thing that attacked Wanda Carver?"

"And maybe Katherine Wetherly, too? I don't know. Something bad, but . . . I don't know."

Lucy climbed out of the truck. She'd taken only a few steps when she turned back to look at her friend.

"Dakota, I don't think I could handle it if something happened to you."

"You could handle it. You could handle anything." Dakota regarded her with a pensive frown. She pulled her silly hat down to her eyes. She pulled her ridiculous scarf up over her nose. "And anyway, nothing's going to happen to me. I'm in disguise."

20

Lucy hadn't planned to stop at the mausoleum.

After everything that had happened yesterday, this was the last place on earth she should be.

And yet she couldn't help herself.

She paused a moment to look in the direction of the truck; she waved, just to let Dakota know she was okay. Hoisting the backpack over her other shoulder, she stepped inside the gates.

"*Lucy . . .*"

Gasping, Lucy whirled around. No one was there behind her, but she could have sworn she'd heard someone say her name. *Dakota?* She paused in the threshold and peered off across the cemetery. She couldn't see the truck, and she didn't hear a sound.

You're doing it again, letting this place get to you.

What was it that Jared had said to her just

yesterday? *"Hurry . . . before it comes back . . ."*

But there was nothing here now to be afraid of. No sense of danger like she'd felt before, no feeling of being watched . . .

Yet without warning, goose bumps crept over her arms. She could feel the hairs lifting at the back of her neck.

The enclosure was soft with shadows. Even on the sunniest of days, the narrow doorway and one grimy window afforded only a pale glow of light. Lucy hated to think of Byron here, in this dank and desolate tomb.

The mausoleum had space for nine bodies.

Every wall—except for the entrance—contained three individual crypts, each one large enough to accommodate a casket.

Byron's was to the right of the doorway, at the very bottom of the wall.

Once a coffin had been placed in its compartment, the opening was then sealed, and a name was engraved on the slab.

Byron had no epitaph.

His name—like those interred here long before him—revealed nothing about the life he had lived, or the person he had been.

Fighting tears, Lucy began walking toward his resting place.

Everything was just as it had been the day before—wind-strewn leaves, dark spatters across the walls, torn clumps of fur . . .

Only now the dark pool of Jared's blood seemed larger than Lucy remembered.

Frowning, she squatted down to examine it more closely.

It flowed in a wide, thick swath—spreading all the way to Byron's crypt. It had frozen there at the base of the slab and oozed down between the cracks in the foundation.

There was a bloody handprint beneath Byron's name.

The fingers were long and splayed, as though desperately reaching for something.

And on the floor beneath it lay a white rose.

Lucy gazed at it and shivered.

It had frozen in the perfection of early bloom, though its stem was wilted now, and its leaves hopelessly shriveled.

The soft creamy petals were stained with blood.

With a gesture that was almost reverent, she reached out her hand to touch it, then drew back again with a surprised cry as a thorn pricked her finger.

Her eyes went uneasily to the handprint.

Jared's hand, she told herself. While she'd left him alone yesterday to look for a hiding place, he'd tried to steady himself against the wall, tried to brace himself against his pain.

That's all it was.

That's all.

Lucy stood up again and sucked her finger. For one moment—and despite the thorns—she was halfway tempted to keep the rose for herself. But then, as an instant wave of guilt came over her, she knew she couldn't.

Someone had obviously left it here for Byron.

A simple gesture of love and remembrance.

An offering of beauty in an atmosphere of death.

She promised herself that when it got warmer, she'd come back here and clean everything up—wash the floor and window, bring fresh flowers, maybe even put a fresh coat of paint on the walls. She'd make it pretty, take some of the dinginess away, and—

"Lucy . . ."

Her heart froze. Her throat closed around a silent scream. She spun to face the doorway, but again, no one was there.

Lucy raced out into the graveyard. She looked frantically in every direction, but saw only Dakota, who was wading clumsily toward her through the snow.

"Did you call me?" Lucy demanded.

Dakota waved both arms in the air. "What?"

"I said, did you *call* me?"

Dakota's long scarf trailed behind her like a rainbow. She frowned, lifted the earflaps on her cap, and cupped one hand around an ear. *"What?"*

"Did you just call my name?" Lucy practically shouted.

The girl stopped and tried to catch her breath. "No. And I thought you were trying to sneak into the church."

"I was, but—"

"Well, you don't have to now." Taking the backpack, Dakota grabbed Lucy's hand and began pulling her back the way they'd come.

"Why not? What are you doing?"

Dakota looked pleased with herself. "I just found another way in."

21

"Here we go, Lucy—talk about luck."

Dakota pulled her truck up in front of the church. An old station wagon was angled against the curb, and as she turned off the motor, she gave Lucy a thumbs-up.

"And why is this lucky?" Lucy wanted to know.

"'Cause this is Mrs. Dempsey's car. I saw it on my way to get coffee."

"Are you insane?"

"While I distract her, you can pretend like you have to use the bathroom and sneak downstairs."

Lucy rolled her eyes. "And of course she won't suspect anything."

"I'll just get her to complain about something. She won't even notice you've left."

Unconvinced, Lucy followed Dakota into the church. Mrs. Dempsey was standing in one of the side aisles, clutching a mop and glaring at the floor.

"I thought I recognized your car outside." Dakota waved one end of her scarf. "How are you, Mrs. Dempsey?"

The cleaning woman squinted at them through the gloom. "Who's that?"

"Us," Dakota replied. She grabbed Lucy's hand and hauled her between some pews. "Can we use your bathroom, please?"

"Go home and use your own."

"It's an emergency."

"I'll show you an emergency. Just look at all the snow that blew in. Melting all over the floor. Ruining everything in sight."

Lucy glanced dubiously around the church, wondering what there was to ruin.

"It'll take me all winter to clean up this mess," Mrs. Dempsey went on, shaking her mop at them. "As if I had nothing better to do!"

Dakota stamped the snow from her shoes, only adding to the puddles. "Bathroom, please?"

"Oh, for heaven's sake. All you young people

ever think about is yourselves. Through that door there, and down the hall to your left. I don't know why you'd need a backpack though."

"She likes her own brand of toilet paper," Dakota explained in a conspiratorial whisper.

Throwing Dakota a grateful look, Lucy made her exit.

It took her a while to find her way back to the cellar.

With her usual poor sense of direction, she made several wrong turns before finally locating the closet with the door at the back.

She pulled out her flashlight and made her way carefully down the stairs, pausing at the bottom to get her bearings. The passageway was just as narrow and spooky as she remembered, and she forced herself not to run. When she reached the door, she'd knocked softly, then waited for a response.

"Jared?"

There was no answer.

"Jared? Are you okay?"

Suddenly apprehensive, she inched open the door. Almost as though she expected something bad to be waiting—and listening—on the other side.

"Jared? It's Lucy."

The first thing she noticed was the smell. Not the underground mustiness of a basement, but a smell like copper, flowing delicately through her nostrils and lingering at the back of her throat. She closed her eyes and tasted it. She swallowed it down, and then it was gone.

Feeling strangely light-headed, Lucy moved forward into the room. Jared was sleeping right where she'd left him, on his back beneath the covers, with his face turned toward the wall. She ran the flashlight beam over him and walked cautiously to the side of the bed. One of his arms lay outstretched on the floor, his hand clenched in a fist.

She realized at once that he was dreaming.

Quick, sharp spasms wracked his body, and wordless sounds mumbled from his lips. As Lucy gazed down at him, he tossed and struggled, locked in battle with some ferocious nightmare.

"Jared, it's all right," she soothed him. "It's just a bad dream."

She thought once more how much he looked like Byron.

And maybe it was because she'd just been to Byron's grave, or that she and Dakota had been talking about him so much lately—but in that moment, touching Jared, Lucy closed her eyes and pretended.

Pretended that things were different. That time had spun backward and fates had been altered. That Byron had managed to touch her hand in the last moment of his life, and broken the spell of what was to come.

"Byron," she whispered.

And that's when she heard the voice.

His voice. *Byron's voice.*

She heard it so clearly, knowing it *had* to be inside her own head, except it seemed so *real*, a real, living voice, coming from two places at once—from inside her head and from Jared's lips.

"Soon, Lucy . . . soon . . ."

Jumping back, she stared down with horrified eyes. Jared was still very much asleep. His body was quiet, his breathing calm.

I didn't hear Byron. It was only in my mind.

Thoroughly unnerved, she checked Jared's bandage. As the gauze fell away, she could see what little remained of his wound now—just a long, narrow swelling down the length of his rib cage.

I didn't hear Byron . . .

She ran her fingertips lightly over Jared's side. She felt the slow, smooth tensing of his muscles . . . she heard his breath catch softly in his throat.

For a split second she felt trapped there, trapped and helplessly paralyzed—trapped by eyes she couldn't see, by instincts she couldn't fathom.

I heard him because I wished it so much . . .

But it was only in my mind.

She left the clothes and food at Jared's bedside.

And recoiled from every shadow as she hurried back upstairs.

22

Maybe I do need a nice long rest.

Lucy stared down at the medicine bottle in her hand.

And maybe hearing Byron's voice was just a side effect of post-traumatic stress.

But she hadn't taken her pills today—hadn't, in fact, for *several* days, though Irene certainly didn't know that. Still . . . it took a while for the medication to get out of your system, didn't it? A few days? *Great. Maybe Jared's part of my syndrome, too.*

Sighing heavily, Lucy set down the bottle and checked the clock on her nightstand. She began pacing back and forth in the bedroom, like a caged animal.

There'd been a message from Matt on the answering machine when she got back home, confirming his appointment with Irene at eight o'clock tonight.

Nothing to be nervous about. It's only my future.

Her stomach was in knots just thinking about it. To be away from Irene would be great enough—to be out of this horrible house, and in a place that actually had some warmth and emotion in it, would seem like heaven.

The doorbell rang, and she let out a yelp.

She'd never get used to being alone in this stupid house—she'd never feel secure, no matter how many locks or alarms.

Matt. Thank goodness.

She'd almost forgotten he was coming early. As she ran down the stairs, she fought a sudden wave of nervousness and tried to convince herself that this time everything would be okay. This time she had real proof to show Matt—not just some wild story she couldn't back up. In fact, she'd checked the bushes as soon as she got home tonight—just to make sure the headstone was still there, hidden beside the porch.

If someone was intent on stealing it—just to make her look crazy—they'd have to be awfully strong and work awfully fast.

Squinting through the peephole, Lucy smiled and opened the door. He looked very much the priest tonight in his official clothes and collar. If *he* couldn't sway Irene, Lucy thought, no one could.

"Am I early enough?" Matt grinned. "Am I intimidating enough?"

"Yes to both. And look down to your left. There in those bushes. That's where I hid it."

She watched the humor fade slowly from his face. He dropped lightly to the ground and parted the evergreens with both hands. Then he stood for several moments without speaking.

"See?" Lucy said quietly. "I didn't make it up."

His glance was immediate—and regretful. "Lucy, I—"

"It doesn't matter about the other time. It was real, and I saw it—but when *you* went to the car, and the stuff was gone—*that* was real, too. I'm just glad you're seeing *this*."

Matt's expression was clearly troubled. "And the delivery truck was unmarked?"

"It was a van. A black van. It didn't have a sign or a name—and the driver was dressed in black, too."

"Nothing on the uniform?"

"No"

"Did you get a good look at his face?"

Just remembering it made her shudder. "He was pale. Angular face . . . his features were bony and sort of sharp. He had deep-set eyes."

"And you're sure you never saw him before?"

"I'm sure."

"Even on the sidewalk, maybe? In a store? Someone you might have passed in a car?"

"I think I would have remembered that face."

"So you'd remember it if you saw it again?"

Lucy nodded. "It was . . . creepy."

"Not someone around school?"

"No. Much older."

"Lucy." As Matt sighed and shook his head, Lucy knew he was scolding her again. "I just wish you'd called the police right away."

"But I told you why I didn't. If I can't get *you* to believe me, why would *they*?"

She hadn't meant to sound so sarcastic, but Matt gave an audible wince. He covered the headstone with the bushes again, then boosted himself back onto the porch.

"I'm considering options," he said.

"What options? The police are treating me like a criminal—the kids at school are treating me like a leper. If I show this to anybody, it's just one more reason to suspect me of . . . whatever everybody suspects me of."

"Lucy, nobody's gonna think you did anything to Angela. That's ridiculous."

"But they'll wonder why the headstone was delivered to me. And why I didn't report it that night." Folding her arms across her chest, Lucy shrank back against the wall. "Nothing I say will make sense to them. And why should it? It doesn't make sense to me either."

"Hey. Stop."

"And with everything else happening, I think part of me really *wanted* to believe it was a joke, except now I don't think it's a joke at all, I don't think it was *ever* supposed to be a joke—"

"Stop. It's okay."

"It's not okay. Somebody sent that to me, and I think they did it because they wanted me to know Angela's dead."

Matt's hands settled firmly on her shoulders. He leaned down until his face was even with her own.

"That's why you *have* to tell the police. For all you know, it could even be connected to Wanda Carver's murder. At the very least—"

Matt broke off, his expression grim. He let go of Lucy's shoulders and gestured adamantly toward the bushes.

"At the very least," he continued, "someone knows who you are and where you live and how to scare you. And maybe it *isn't* anything more than just some perverted joke. But . . . are you willing to take that chance?"

Lucy hesitated. "But what if—"

"I'm not. I'm not willing to take that chance."

He held her in a silent stare. As Lucy gazed back at him, he lifted one hand slowly toward her face.

"I'm not, Lucy."

A glare of headlights suddenly swung into the driveway and raked across them on the porch. Without missing a beat, Matt hastily made the sign of the cross in front of Lucy's nose.

"Bless you, my child." He winked, but without a smile. "And don't worry, I'll take care of it."

23

The world seemed almost beautiful tonight, Lucy thought.

Matt had reassured her that he could talk Irene into anything. And he'd promised to take care of the headstone. And as Lucy drove through the quiet streets toward Pine Corners, she realized that the snow had stopped falling and that stars were scattered brilliantly across the sky.

She'd told Irene she was meeting Dakota at the bookstore to study. Not exactly a lie, Lucy rationalized—Dakota *would* be showing up later, after she went shopping with her mom. And it wasn't as if Irene paid much attention, anyway—the only thing Irene had been concerned about was Angela's car.

"But it started right up," Lucy had reassured

her. "It seems to be running perfectly fine."

"Which doesn't necessarily mean it will start right up and run perfectly fine the next time you try it," Irene had reminded her crisply. "This is a very expensive car, Lucy, and a very good one. You must be abusing it in some way. It never gave Angela one bit of trouble."

Lucy had bit back an angry reply. But only because Matt had made a mimicking face at her over Irene's shoulder.

Now she didn't want to think about Aunt Irene anymore. Or Jared. Or Byron. Or Wanda Carver's murder, or the sheriff's interrogation, or the possibility of some lunatic running loose around Pine Ridge.

She just wanted to go somewhere comforting.

She just wanted to believe that her life might finally be getting better.

The Candlewick Shop was crowded when Lucy got there. Those same wonderful smells of musty books and strong coffee and aged wood greeted her the second she came through the door. Mr. Montana wasn't at his usual spot behind the counter; Lucy could hear him talking and laughing with someone in the adjacent room. She was actually glad to slip in unnoticed. As much as she liked Dakota's father, she didn't really feel like having a conversation tonight.

She wove her way around the store, taking her time. She strolled slowly through each section, up and down each narrow aisle, checking out titles from time to time, taking down a book to browse through it. But as the small rooms began to grow more and more packed with customers, Lucy finally headed upstairs.

Disappointingly, she found the second floor nearly as busy as the first. After squeezing herself in and out of several more cramped rooms, she escaped to the the last and tiniest one.

Supernatural section, she realized. *Dakota's favorite.*

To her surprise—and relief—there weren't as many people in here. Probably because it was so claustrophobic, she reasoned, with its impossible maze of tall shelves, nooks and crannies, and dead ends.

Dakota's favorite. Dakota's passion.

Pausing inside the doorway, Lucy scanned the overflowing collection of books. She could still remember when Dakota had shown her all these, and the conversation they'd had at the time.

"Some people call it supernatural," Dakota had told her. "Some call it real. There are just so many things out there that can't be explained or understood—not by our limited human perceptions, anyway. But those things still exist. They still happen. People are still affected by them . . . destinies are still controlled by them."

"Is that what you believe?" Lucy had been both curious and fascinated with the discussion. "That our destinies are predetermined?"

"I believe in everything," Dakota had answered. "But the question is . . . what do *you* believe in? Just because you can't see what's in front of you doesn't mean it's not there."

Lucy sidestepped a reader and moved slowly down the first row of shelves. She'd been right to confide in Dakota, she told herself—it had been absolutely the right thing to do. Dakota hadn't flinched at Lucy's confessions—Dakota hadn't seemed shocked or scared or even all that surprised.

Dakota believed in everything.

And Dakota would keep Lucy grounded.

With a sudden rush of gratitude, Lucy wished her friend would hurry and get here. She felt better with Dakota around. She felt almost like a sane, normal person.

"Is that her?"

The voice spoke softly and at a distance. In fact, Lucy didn't even pay attention to it until she heard the question repeated, and then the muffled laughter that followed.

"Don't touch any books in here. You might get the Lucy Curse."

Startled, Lucy spun toward the door and saw two girls huddled together, whispering. Instantly she recognized them from school and assumed they were whispering about her.

Her face flushed with embarrassment. Realizing they'd been caught, the girls ducked their heads, giggled again, and quickly disappeared.

Lucy felt sick. Just what she'd feared would happen was actually happening. Were the whispered insults and superstitions outside of school now? All over town? How could she keep going, day after day, knowing how everyone felt about her and trying to act as if it didn't hurt?

Slipping to the end of the aisle, she busied herself skimming through books. Top to bottom, left to right, pretending to read every title. Perhaps at one time they'd been categorized, but now there was just a messy and double-shelved hodgepodge of subjects that were mostly alien to her.

Witchcraft. The occult. Time travel. Ghosts and spiritualism, vampires and werewolves. Death, near-death, and how to talk with the dead. More myths and legends than she'd ever known existed. Satanism. Magic. Dreams and astrology and Tarot cards.

From time to time Lucy glanced around, alert for more whispers. The customers were dwindling now, and the upstairs area was quiet, except for an occasional sniffle and shuffling of feet. *Isolated incident,* she told herself, *no need to get all paranoid.* But in her heart she knew better. In her heart, she knew that facing the kids at school was only going to get worse.

Making her way down yet another aisle, Lucy

continued exploring. Symbols and talismans. Zombies. Rituals and secret societies. Haunted houses. Unexplained disappearances. Mysterious ships and lighthouses. Human sacrifice. The history of Evil.

Lucy nervously checked over her shoulder and peeked around the end of the aisle. A scholarly looking gentleman was still in here, and a woman in a purple velvet cape, and three college guys who were taking notes. One of them lifted his head and leered at her, and she moved farther back into the labyrinth of shelves.

She wondered what time it was. It must be almost closing time, she figured, and Dakota still hadn't shown up. Well, she'd wait just a little while longer. Pull out some homework and try to get something done. As she rounded the last row, she spotted a brick-manteled niche in the wall—what might once have been a large fireplace—but was now empty and perfect for studying. She opened her backpack and took out her history assignment. Then she spread out some papers to sit on, wedged herself into the opening, and began to read.

It was warm in here, and she hadn't bothered

to take off her jacket. As she flipped back and forth through her textbook, her head began to nod. She was so sleepy all of a sudden, she could hardly keep her eyes open. *Just for a minute*, she thought . . . *I'll finish this page, then I'll close my eyes just for a minute.* Dakota would be here anytime now. Even if she happened to doze off, Dakota would find her and wake her up . . .

Lucy was asleep almost at once.

Before she'd even read another word.

Asleep and blissfully unaware of anything else around her . . . oblivious to the minutes creeping by.

It was the silence, she decided later.

The vast, crushing silence that finally woke her—penetrating her subconscious with a troubled sense of something not quite right.

The room was pitch-dark. For one terrifying second, she didn't know where she was. Starting up in panic, she smacked her head against something sharp, and stars burst softly behind her eyes.

The bookstore! Calm down—you're in the bookstore—you fell asleep . . .

Moaning, Lucy felt her head. Her hair was

wet and sticky, her scalp already beginning to swell. A trickle of blood oozed over her forehead and into one eye, and she angrily wiped it away.

She remembered now—sitting down, studying, nodding off. This time she was more careful straightening up. She reached for the top of the opening, to the border of bricks where she'd hit her head. She hesitated, and she listened.

No one was in the room with her now.

And it didn't sound as though anyone was in the entire building.

What happened to Dakota?

Still feeling slightly dizzy, Lucy braced one hand against the bricks and shoved herself out. She stood for a moment on wobbly knees, then began searching for the door. If she could just get to the light switch, she'd feel a whole lot better. Even though she was pretty sure now that she was locked in here all alone.

"Mr. Montana?" she yelled.

Why hadn't he woken her up and sent her home? Why hadn't *anybody* woken her up and sent her home?

"Mr. Montana? Is anybody there?"

Lucy was determined to stay calm. As she made her way painstakingly through the maze of aisles and shelves, she reminded herself that this was no big deal, that all she had to do was use her cell phone and call Dakota to come and rescue her. It had probably happened lots of times, people being overlooked and locked in. With the crazy way this place was laid out, how could it *not* have happened before? She'd even managed to find the humor in her situation until she reached the door.

Reached the door and found it locked.

It didn't make sense. She knew the door had been wide open when she'd first come in and sat down—why would anyone close and lock it after hours?

Lucy fought down a fresh wave of fear. She ran her hand along the wall, feeling for the light switch.

She flipped it on, but nothing happened.

The dark seemed to swallow her whole.

"Mr. Montana!" Lucy banged on the door as hard as she could and shouted even louder. "Mr. Montana—*somebody*—*please* let me out!"

Her heart was pounding in her throat, filling her ears with panic. She flattened herself against the wall and tried desperately to think.

You have your cell phone. And a flashlight is still in your backpack. Turn on the flashlight, make the call, pull yourself together, and wait.

Fumbling blindly, she groped her way back to the corner. She forgot where she'd left her backpack, so when she tripped over it without warning, she fell sideways against the fireplace opening. She heard the painful crash of her shoulder, her feet scrambling for balance, and then something else.

A flat, heavy thud of something falling.

As though a book—or something like a book—had dropped onto the floor.

Lucy felt an immediate upsweep of dust, and backed away from it, coughing. She dug through her backpack, found the flashlight at the bottom, and quickly turned it on.

It *was* a book.

And even at first glance, Lucy could sense that it was unique.

It was of medium size—five inches wide, perhaps, and no more than eight inches in length—but it was extremely thick. The leather binding was brittle and cracked with age, ragged around the edges. The book was caked in dust and mold. A shroud of spiderwebs held it shut, and dampness had disfigured the front and back covers, leaving black sores of decay along the spine.

Even to Lucy's unpracticed eye, it was obvious that this book had been long abandoned and utterly forgotten.

Approaching cautiously, Lucy shone her flashlight over the opening in the wall. She could see now where several bricks had come loose where she'd fallen against them, leaving a deep gap in the mantel.

A hiding place. A secret hiding place.

In spite of the circumstances, Lucy's heart quickened with excitement. What else *could* it be but a hiding place? Someone had taken great pains to conceal this book inside that mantel, no telling how many years ago. But who? And why?

She wondered if Mr. Montana or Dakota knew about it. If *anyone* in Pine Ridge knew about it. Probably not, or else it would be in somebody's personal library right now. Or on one of these cluttered bookshelves, waiting to be sold.

Still, Lucy hesitated to pick it up. She stood over it for several more moments, illuminating it with the flashlight, peering down at its cover. Was that a title, barely visible beneath all that dust? Or some sort of design?

She didn't even realize she was holding her breath.

She knew there was something extraordinary about this book. Something different . . . something . . .

Lucy chewed doubtfully on her lip. *What?* What was it about this tattered old book that made her feel such a sense of . . .

Reverence.

It came to her, like a gentle whisper.

Reverence. Power.

Very slowly, Lucy knelt down. She held the flashlight in one hand and reached for the book with the other.

She was trembling.

Reverence . . . power . . .

Destiny.

24

She completely forgot about making the phone call.

About being alone, about being frightened, about being locked in.

In fact, once Lucy had gathered enough courage to pick up the book, she made herself comfortable on the floor and slowly began to examine her treasure.

At first the book wouldn't open.

As though after all this time, it still resisted being discovered and revealed.

It had taken both time and patience, working her fingers beneath the cover, prying oh so carefully, until at last, and with an almost audible sigh, the book parted itself in her hands.

Using her sleeve, Lucy wiped most of the dust away. She was able to see the cover more clearly now, but she still couldn't make it out. The title had practically disappeared, and the few engraved letters remaining were a language that was foreign to her. She touched the letters with one fingertip, delicately tracing each shape. They seemed almost regal—as if connected to some grand and glorious past.

The text, however, was different. No words had been boldly engraved here—instead, these lines and lines of writing had been done by hand, most probably with a quill. The ink was badly faded—in some spots, hopelessly invisible. Many of the pages had crumbled at their edges, or been carelessly torn, or even completely ripped out. Some bore the marks of fingerprints, or water spots, or candlewax, or burns. And here and there along the margins, a tiny sketch had been added, or an odd design, a sequence of numbers, or what might have been a spontaneous note.

A journal? A manual? Some sort of logbook?

Thoroughly intrigued, Lucy searched on.

There was far more than just writing here, she soon realized. She found maps of places she couldn't identify, drawings of plants she'd never seen. Long-pressed flowers and leaves, now turned to dust. And an occasional spattering of brownish drops that reminded her of blood . . .

What is *this?*

The more pages Lucy turned, the more eager she was for answers. Whose book had this been, and what had become of the owner? How had the book ended up here, and why had it been hidden away? How many years ago had it been written? What secrets did it hold? Lucy felt as though she were strangely and suddenly obsessed with it—she couldn't rest until its mysteries were solved.

She held the flashlight closer. She'd totally forgotten her fear, how frantic she'd been to get out of the bookstore. And she had no intentions of leaving now—not when she wasn't even halfway through the book. Turning another page, Lucy stared down at the sharp, slanted writing. Like swift slashes upon the page. *Male*, she thought, though she wasn't sure why. She liked his penmanship. She tried to imagine his hand moving over the paper, and she moved her hand over it, too.

A strong hand, this writer of words—a strong and gentle and merciless hand . . .

Her cell phone rang, shattering the silence.

Lucy screamed and jumped, and fumbled into her pocket.

"Hello?"

"Lucy! Where are you?"

"Dakota?" Darkness engulfed her as she dropped the flashlight. She lunged for it across the floor.

"Lucy, what are you *doing*? And where *are* you? My dad just called, and said Irene just called *him*, and—"

"Wait a minute. Where are *you*?"

"Out in the middle of nowhere. Picking up my brother from my aunt and uncle's house. Because my brother and my cousin are both idiots, and they drove my brother's car onto a frozen pond. Which turned out not to be as frozen as it looked."

"Are they okay?" The flashlight stopped rolling. It flickered once, went out, then glowed again dimly.

"For now. However, my brother's fate is subject to change the minute my dad gets ahold of him.

We're on our way back to town, even as I speak."

"What did your dad tell Irene?"

"To call me."

"So what did *you* tell her?"

"That you were with me, but you were in the bathroom and couldn't come to the phone."

"I owe you one. I owe you many."

"You owe me nothing. It's my absolute pleasure to protect you from Irene."

"Thanks," Lucy smiled. "What time is it?"

"Almost midnight."

"Midnight!" Retrieving her flashlight, Lucy plopped back down. She couldn't find the book. It must have fallen when she'd gone after the flashlight, but now she couldn't see it anywhere.

"Lucy, how come you didn't meet me?"

"I *did* meet you. In fact, that's where I am right now. Locked in your store."

Dakota's reply was a long, confused silence.

"I said, I'm locked in your store." Where was the book? It had to be here somewhere—it couldn't have fallen that far.

"But I looked for you. And Dad said you hadn't come in."

"He didn't see me. I fell asleep studying, and when I woke up, everyone was gone."

"So where are you now?"

"In your favorite room . . . sort of in the fireplace."

"Oh, yeah? I like that spot, too. No wonder nobody found you." Dakota gave a tolerant sigh. "Look, it might take me a while to get there—it is supposed to start sleeting tonight."

Lucy made an uninterested sound into the phone. She was trying to shine the flashlight, hold on to the phone, and feel around the floor at the same time.

"Look, you should probably just come home with me," Dakota went on. "Since you don't really know how to drive on ice. But these roads are really bad out here, so if I don't think I can make it within the next hour, I'll call my dad and just have him pick you up, okay? Oh, and he always turns the shop thermostat down at night—so if you're cold, feel free to make coffee."

"I would, but I'm locked in," Lucy mumbled.

"So what does that have to do with making coffee?"

"No, I mean I'm locked in this room. And the lights don't work."

Dakota paused. Lucy aimed the flashlight toward the empty fireplace.

"What do you mean?" Dakota asked. "None of those doors have locks on them."

25

Lucy didn't realize that her phone had gone dead.

That her hand was trembling, that the flashlight beam was wavering off through the shadows.

"None of those rooms have locks . . ."

Suddenly she felt the cold. She'd been so warm and comfortable before, so engrossed in the book, but now she was absolutely freezing.

She was afraid to go near the door.

Afraid to go near that door that held her prisoner . . .

"None of those rooms have locks."

But she'd tried the door, and it hadn't opened; she'd tried the knob, and it hadn't turned. *It must have been me then . . . the door must be stuck . . . I should have pushed it harder.*

Swallowing a taste of fear, Lucy listened again through the silence.

She listened to the old building creak and settle around her, to the drafts seeping up through the floor.

It sounded almost like footsteps.

Footsteps out in the hallway. Footsteps coming closer.

Lucy's grip tightened around the flashlight. She shut it off and sat there trembling in the dark.

Please, Dakota, please hurry . . .

She told herself that the footsteps weren't real, that the bookstore was safe, that nobody was in here except her. She told herself to quit being so ridiculous, to get up, to move. Go downstairs. Wait for Dakota.

But she *couldn't* move. She couldn't stop shaking.

And something was breathing now . . .

Short puffs of air, on the other side of that door.

A snuffling sound moving back and forth along the door, a gutteral sound creeping low across the floor.

She could hear it pause to sniff the air . . .

She could hear it trying to get in.

Oh God . . . oh my God . . .

She squeezed herself tight into the corner. She hugged her knees to her chest and pressed her head back against the wall.

The doorknob rattled softly.

No . . . please no . . .

There was a sharp clicking sound along the floorboards . . . a long scraping sound across the door . . .

Then something thumped hard against it.

Something strong enough to shake it in its frame and cause the room to shiver all around her.

Go away . . . go away!

The door began to open. Inch by torturous inch.

Teasing her . . . taking its time.

She would use the flashlight, she told herself. Use it as a weapon—strike first, think later. She had the advantage of darkness on her side—she was well hidden—she could use the element of surprise.

But now she realized the thing was coming toward her.

Step by muffled step, up and down the narrow aisles, between the crooked shelves, it was coming *toward* her, directly and stealthily toward the exact spot where she hid.

It knows I'm here, she realized.

It's known all along.

Reason deserted her. In that instant, self-preservation kicked in with such force that Lucy was on her feet before she even realized. She let out a shout of fear and rage. And she threw herself so hard, so fast, against the closest bookshelf that she didn't have time to feel the pain.

The bookshelf went over.

With a deafening crash, the rickety bookshelf toppled forward, spilling its entire contents and crashing down to the floor.

Then . . . silence.

Silence and blessed emptiness.

Because whatever had come for her was gone now.

And Lucy knew it would not come back tonight.

26

She should still be terrified.

Lucy sat on the overstuffed couch by the front window of the bookshop. Sleet scratched against the glass and whirled through the courtyard in a silvery frenzy.

Of *course* she should still be terrified, she kept telling herself. After what had just happened upstairs . . .

But I'm not.

Shocked, yes. Bewildered, yes. Badly shaken, yes.

But not terrified.

She curled up on the cushions and watched the weather. A few of the wind chimes—those not yet frozen—were bouncing on the clothesline, clanging merrily away. Lucy felt a smile tug at the corners of her mouth.

She could still hear the crash of the bookshelf hitting the floor.

She could still hear the explosion of books going in all directions.

And whatever had been skulking there in the dark had probably been caught right in the middle of everything.

But now it was gone.

Lucy still wasn't sure how she knew this. How she could tell from the very feel of the air around her that she was alone now, and safe. That there was no longer a threat in the shadows, or a reason to panic and hide.

She just *knew*.

And right now she didn't want to think beyond that or understand it or try to figure it out.

Right now, just the knowing was enough.

Pleasing, somehow. And liberating.

A part of me. It's becoming a normal part of me. It's who I am.

The realization surprised her a little, but she found it comforting, too. And curiously intriguing, just like the book she held in her arms.

Lucy turned her attention from the courtyard. Dakota had warned her it would take a while to get here, but Lucy didn't mind anymore. She didn't even mind that the electricity seemed to be off in the whole shop. Winter shone in through the windowpane, bathing her in a pale glow. She didn't bother with the flashlight now—somehow the reading seemed better without it.

If only I knew what it said—if only I could figure it out!

Cradling the book against her chest, she rested her chin against it. It was maddening not being able to decipher these words, these maps, these cryptic symbols she felt herself so totally drawn to. She couldn't shake the feeling that there were great and wondrous secrets hidden between the pages, and a world of revelations beyond any imagining.

Like an enchanted fairy tale, she concluded.

So maybe I've been bewitched.

The idea amused her. She put the book in her lap, opened the cover, and resumed her search.

Page after page of the unknown language. Page after page of the sketches and notes. Maybe there was someone who could actually translate it, Lucy thought. Maybe someone at the university. Maybe she could ask Irene. Or maybe Matt or Father Paul would know.

But I won't tell them much. I won't give anything away. This is my book.

Frowning, Lucy paused. Of course, it wasn't her book—she'd found it upstairs, it belonged to Mr. Montana.

Didn't it?

But after all, *she* was the one who'd discovered it. If it hadn't been for her, who knew how many more years or centuries would pass before anyone ever found it? In fact, the book had probably been here long before Mr. Montana even owned the shop. And to be even more precise, it had been hidden in the fireplace mantel—who knew *where* that mantel had originally come from?

Yes . . . the mantel . . .

Lucy hadn't considered this before, but it opened up a whole new range of possibilities. Scarcely able to contain her excitement, she tried to get back to her reading.

Strong, beautiful letters . . . and . . . sensitivity . . . but fear . . . resignation . . . time is running out . . . and someone must know the truth . . .

She wasn't sure exactly when it happened—or when she fully became aware of it. Her fingertip gliding beneath each sentence on the page . . . her lips reading the foreign words aloud . . . her mind seeing them in English.

It was almost like the slow lifting of a curtain, the gradual letting in of light, the shadows melting away. For suddenly, Lucy realized that the words in front of her were making sense, and that she could understand what some of them meant.

Her eyes began to widen. Her finger moved from word to word, pointing, going faster—sentence to sentence, paragraph to paragraph, page after page. As in her visions, there was no complete, unbroken narrative—but rather bits and pieces, a comment here, a phrase there, and through it all, the slow emergence of a dark, disturbing theme . . .

. . . *during daylight* . . .

. . . *handsome young man* . . .

. . . *transform* . . .

. . . *wolf or large black dog* . . .

Lucy couldn't stop. Her fingers fairly flew across the pages.

She could read it, though the words made no real sense to her. And with every brief touch, something seemed to stir within her heart. Sorrow? Familiarity? Longing? Lucy couldn't tell, though at some deeper, more instinctive level, she felt that some connection had been made.

But she was growing tired. Her hands were beginning to shake; her head was aching. Whatever had happened just now had taken far more out of her than she'd realized. Despite her fascination, she knew she had to rest.

One more . . . just one.

And so she turned just one page farther.

And felt the shock go through her like a knife.

There before her was a sketch of an angel.

An angel with no face.

An angel that cradled a rotting skull beneath its great, soft wings . . .

No . . . it can't be . . .

She'd seen that angel before.

Seen four of them, in fact.

Guarding each corner of Byron's mausoleum.

Lucy's strength drained out of her in a rush.

She wanted to look away, but she couldn't.

Her eyes went over every detail of the featureless face, the mighty wings, the macabre skull. Something had been written just beneath them—sharp, slanted letters much larger, much bolder, than all the others. And even though her stamina was spent, Lucy knew she had no choice—she *had* to know the meaning of these words.

She pressed her trembling fingers to the page. And in her mind, the mystery fell away.

MY SON . . .

MOST POWERFUL OF THE UNDEAD.

27

He would have to feed, and feed soon.

It was the only way he could heal completely, gain back his strength.

His physical wounds had mended, as they always did. And though he had managed to exist for a while on what was convenient and readily available, it was not the nourishment his soul demanded.

He had never lacked for prey before, never known starvation.

Bus stops had proved to be natural, never-ending sources. Homeless shelters, soup kitchens, and abandoned buildings. Filthy street corners and flophouses, subways and subterranean tunnels—all havens for the hopeless and indigent, the ones never missed or mourned.

Blood banks were a little trickier, of course. And hospitals always required that extra bit of caution, though he had certainly foraged enough of them through the years with no mishaps whatsoever.

Nursing homes were no challenge at all.

And grave robbing was a delicate art he had long ago honed to sheer perfection. That consummate mixture of skill and timing and speed—the undetected rearranging of soil and spoiling flowers. With or without blood, the flesh was still tasty. All worth the risk taking, all worth the thrill.

Just thinking of it now made him ravenous.

His pace lengthened, and his body flowed.

He prowled a quiet neighborhood, past house after house of locked doors that could never keep him out. He briefly considered returning to the park, then decided against it. Not wise to strike in the same location again so soon—better to keep a low profile, at least for a few more nights.

Breathing deeply of the raw, cold air, he detected the scent of . . .

Child.

Small child . . . boy child . . .

He frowned and tested the air again.

He'd never been keen on children—only when there was no other possible way, only when his hand was forced, only in the most dire and desperate of circumstances. And even then, he was always left with a half-empty feeling, a sense of discontent.

This child was still three blocks away; he had two young parents with him, and an old grandfather, and a dog.

No, he decided impatiently, even as hunger pains ripped through his belly. No . . . even as he started to salivate . . .

No. *Too much trouble for too little satisfaction.*

Swiftly he ran in the opposite direction, his thoughts on survival, his thoughts on Lucy.

His body quivered, and his hunger grew.

She had drawn him there tonight, to the old bookshop, to the old part of town. With the first oozing of blood from that cut on her scalp, his body had craved, and his appetite surged. She had not known, of course, and the wound was inconsequential at worst. But still, he had needed to see for himself that she was safe and relatively unharmed.

Once reassured, it had amused him to stand against the door and shut her in. To make the creaking sounds upon the floor. To hear the growing panic in her voice, until every crack and crevice of the building was filled with Lucy's fear.

He had breathed it in like a prisoner too long without air.

But tonight he had tired very quickly of sport. Even before that bookcase had come crashing down while he'd watched from the safety of the hall.

You'll have to be much quicker than that, Lucy.

Her defiance had excited him and made him restless. His hunger was too great, and the scent of her blood too much a torment. When she was his at last, then he would toy with her as long, and as slowly, as he pleased.

And she would love him for it all the more.

But now he must feed, and feed soon.

Perhaps in the wilderness tonight, outside the confines of the town.

He never forgot how much he missed it, or how good it felt to come back. The silent woods, deep and dark with secrets . . . the hills flowing endlessly toward the stars. Snow unspoiled by plows, and roads that stretched unwalked for miles and miles.

His woods—*his* stars—*his* moonswept sky.

Only now, his moon was hidden by the clouds, and sleet ripped down in razors, slicing his face like scars. He embraced the cold; it stung, and it was bitter. His silky hair, his sinuous shadow, ethereal as smoke . . .

But what was this?

From a distance he saw it, abandoned in a snowbank. It was coated thickly in ice. Old and rusty and undependable, and conveniently unlocked.

He recognized it at once, for he knew this truck well.

Polluting the streets of Pine Ridge, chauffeuring family and friends, parked at the festival, the cemetery, the church. At the soup kitchen and at Lucy's . . .

He opened the door, eyes narrowing.

Ah, yes . . . I see we're out of gas.

And it's quite a long walk back for help.

A *very* long walk, in fact, down these snow-sunken country roads. Where the night lured and confused. Where the sounds of unearthly howling were not always made by the wind. And where uncertain detours led almost certainly to dead ends.

He reached one hand toward the passenger seat.

His lips curled into a smile.

The annoying brother had been here most recently, but Lucy had been here before that. Those moments of laughter were still here—he could sense them. Those rare moments of happiness he so marveled at.

Those moments of happiness he was so seldom a part of . . .

Lifting his head, he sniffed the frozen air, then groaned with an all-consuming hunger.

They were coming back to the truck now, and they were cold and tired.

He slipped inside and crouched low on the seat.

He rested.

And waited

And planned.

28

"So, I hear you're spending this afternoon with Mrs. Wetherly."

"A couple hours, I think."

Lucy tucked the receiver under her chin and tried to pull on her socks.

"Am I good, or what?" Matt teased.

"You're perfect." What was it Dakota always liked to say? *Just because he's a priest doesn't mean he's dead?*

"Then why the glum voice? I thought you'd be bouncing off the walls with joy."

"I . . ." Lucy made a valiant effort to show some enthusiasm. "I'm really happy."

"I've heard happy, and believe me, that's not it." There was a shuffling sound as though he were sifting through papers. "What's going on?"

Tell him about the book. Tell him.

But instead of giving her a chance to answer, Matt asked, "Have you seen Dakota?"

"You mean, today?"

"We were supposed to meet at the soup kitchen this morning, but she never showed up."

Lucy winced. She'd promised to meet Dakota there, too, and she'd completely forgotten about it.

"She might not be home yet. She was at her aunt and uncle's last night, and her dad told her to stay over if the roads were too bad."

"That makes sense."

"I'll have her call you, if I hear from her," Lucy promised. "And thanks, Matt. For setting this up with Gran."

"I'm just glad things worked out so well. So here's the plan. You're supposed to be at her house at noon to have lunch. Mrs. Dempsey's cooking up a feast. And I'm going with you."

"For me? Or for the feast?"

"Hmmm. It's a toss-up."

As another telephone rang in the background, Matt sounded annoyed.

"Lucy, can you hang on for just a second? I

hate to put you on hold, but I need to take this for Father Paul."

"It's okay."

Obligingly, Lucy sat down on her bed and finished pulling up her socks. Matt was right—she *should* be overjoyed about staying with Gran. Yet suddenly, what had been so important to her before didn't seem like such a priority.

Not with that book to think about.

Not with Jared to take care of.

Because of the bad weather, she hadn't been able to see him this morning. She wondered if he was cold and hungry or if his wound had somehow gotten worse. Or if someone had found him. She felt responsible for him; she needed to be there.

She needed to know he was okay.

She needed to know if a *lot* of things were okay.

Come on, Dakota, call me.

She'd already tried Dakota's house five times this morning, but no one had answered.

Call me . . . we have to talk!

Lucy had so much to tell her.

Especially about the book . . .

She'd taken the book with her last night.

And it wasn't as though she'd planned it, either—it had just sort of happened.

She'd been sitting there on the couch in the bookstore, still stunned from the last thing she'd read. She'd seen Mr. Montana hurrying into the courtyard, then bursting through the door on a blast of icy wind. And she'd simply slipped the book into her backpack. Slipped it right in without a second thought.

"Taxi at your service," Mr. Montana had greeted her. "I think I'm supposed to take you home."

"Where's Dakota?"

"Well, she got stuck out at her aunt and uncle's house. Those country roads are impossible in this kind of weather."

"Is she okay?"

"Oh, sure. I told her to just spend the night there. You'd better leave your car, too, Lucy. And keep the doors unlocked so they won't freeze. You girls can come back and pick it up later."

He'd flicked the light switch several times, then frowned.

"Looks like the power's out again. Oh, well. Every single time we have sleet like this."

"I'm really sorry about getting locked in, Mr. Montana."

"Oh, it's happened before. And it'll probably happen again. The worst thing would be if you didn't like books." He'd smiled and ushered her out the door. "Come on, let's get you home."

So she'd taken the book, but she still felt guilty afterward. A little. She told herself it was just a loan; that as soon as she finished with it, she'd return it and hide it back behind the bricks, and no one would ever have to know.

But in her heart, she had no intention of giving it back.

She didn't understand why, exactly.

She just *had* to have that book.

She'd felt so conspicuous in Mr. Montana's car, as though she had "thief" written all over her face. She couldn't wait to get inside and up to her room, but Irene was waiting for her in the living room.

"Lucy, where on earth have you been? I thought you were studying tonight."

Lucy waved good-bye to Mr. Montana. She

shut the front door, shook the sleet off her coat, and stomped her shoes on the mat. "We *were* studying."

"Where's the car? How did you get home?"

"Mr. Montana brought me—he didn't want me driving on the ice. He told me to leave the car and pick it up tomorrow."

She wished Irene would stop talking. She could hardly keep herself from pulling out the book and reading it on the spot.

"Lucy?"

"What?" She'd been so anxious about tonight, about Matt and Irene talking. Discussing her future and a new place to live. But as Lucy stood there holding her backpack, she hadn't been able to concentrate on anything else but the book.

"Lucy, sit down. I want to talk to you."

That's when she'd gotten that sudden, sinking feeling that Matt's visit had all been for nothing. She'd lowered herself onto the couch and braced herself for bad news. She'd thought about the book. Her heart sank to her toes.

"As I'm sure you know," Irene began, "Father Matt and I had quite an interesting talk tonight."

Uh-oh, here it comes . . .

She was used to bad news by now. But the book was in her backpack, and she had to finish reading it. She could hardly keep from fidgeting. She watched Irene's face, but it told her nothing.

"Lucy, I don't want you to think that I'm staying away indefinitely. This job in Paris isn't permanent, you know."

Hesitantly, Lucy nodded.

"I just don't want you to think that . . ." Irene plucked nervously at the sterling silver chain around her throat. "I don't want you to feel that I'm abandoning you."

Wow. Matt must have laid a huge *load of guilt on her tonight.*

This time Lucy shook her head.

"Father Matt thinks this is a wonderful idea, your living with Mrs. Wetherly. A marvelous opportunity for you. And I agree with him."

"You . . . do?"

Lucy had been totally shocked. She'd stared at her aunt with suspicious disbelief.

"And," Irene went on, "it seems to resolve many of my concerns for you. You'll have a safe place to stay, and I'm sure you'll be an enormous help to Mrs. Wetherly. You'll be earning money of your own. And it will certainly give me peace of mind while I'm gone."

Right. Like that was ever an issue.

But Lucy felt too preoccupied to hold a grudge. Relieved about staying with Gran, and stunned by her discoveries in the book, her mind had continued spinning in a dozen different directions.

"Well, it's late," Irene announced. "We both should be getting to bed."

Hardly able to contain herself, Lucy waited while Irene turned off the first-floor lights. Then she followed her aunt up the stairs.

On the landing, Irene paused. She'd looked at Lucy with a frown that was almost defensive. "I'm glad you're home safe," she'd said.

But Lucy scarcely heard. All she could think about was the book.

She locked her bedroom door, got undressed, and put the medallion back in her nightstand. Then she showered in record time, threw on pajamas, and jumped into bed.

She'd been pondering the book all night. Ever since she'd deciphered that last mysterious message.

She'd decided it was a hoax, of course.

It had to be.

The whole idea of "undead" was just too fantastic, too unbelievable.

Someone had made it up, like a ghost story.

Someone had made it up and written it all down to look like a journal. But it wasn't a journal at all—it was a work of pure fiction, just the renderings of a brilliant imagination.

She told herself this as she propped herself up in bed, holding the book open on her lap. She told herself this while at the same time she wondered how she could possibly have read and understood the unknown language it was written in.

And the way I discovered it, hidden away in that mantel . . .

How weird was *that*?

She told herself it was just another prank; she told herself a lot of things.

But the truth was . . . the book was *real*.

The book was *genuine*.

And Lucy had no clue how she knew this.

She just *did*.

She'd found it. And understood it.

And as she sat there flipping slowly through the pages, she summoned all her concentration and touched the letters once more with her fingertips.

Nothing happened.

That's weird . . .

She tried again. She pressed her fingers to the words and held them there, but absolutely nothing came into her head.

No! I didn't imagine it!

She was absolutely certain this time.

In fact, here was the sketch of the faceless angel, and the bold writing beneath it.

Once more she'd focused. Once more she'd touched her fingers to the letters.

Nothing.

What's going on here?

She told herself all she needed was rest.

A good night's sleep to replenish herself by morning.

Yes, that's all it is. A good night's sleep.

Frustrated, she'd closed the book and laid it on her nightstand.

She'd promised herself to wake up refreshed, and then she'd try again.

And this time she would understand every word . . .

"The news is," Matt said, "that Father Paul might be leaving us."

Engrossed in her own thoughts, Lucy said nothing.

"Hey, are you there?"

"Sorry. Yes, I'm here. He's moving?"

"Retiring, I think is how they're putting it."

"So . . . you'll be the only priest now?"

"Looks that way. And don't sound so disappointed. Oh, there goes that phone again. Look, how about I pick you up? Quarter till?"

"Quarter till. And Matt?"

"Hmmm?"

"I really am happy about living with Gran."

"Good. I want that in writing."

She heard the click on Matt's end of the line. She sat there and clutched the receiver.

Writing . . .

What was it Dakota had told her? That she should write everything down? So if she mysteriously died or disappeared, there'd be documentation?

Well, it was time.

Lucy took out a clean notebook and a pen. She sat cross-legged on her bed, and she thought.

At first, she didn't quite know how to start.

"Everything that's happened to you . . . a record of every experience . . ."

And then, finally, she wrote.

Everything.

Just like she'd told Dakota.

29

Lucy wrote all morning—racking her brain, trying to recall every detail.

She wasn't sure why she felt such a sudden need to do this. Maybe it had something to do with finding the book in the mantel. Maybe *that* had inspired her to write her own unbelievable story. Maybe someday someone would read her own personal journal and want to believe it as much as she wanted to *be* believed.

But then again . . . maybe her words would be doubted.

Just as she doubted the words of that strange and magical book. Those words she'd been able to translate.

Those words that hinted of truth.

She didn't realize how much time had passed. Checking the clock, she hid her notebook and hurried downstairs just as Matt rang the bell.

She didn't even have a chance to say hello before he reached out and grabbed her by the shoulders.

"Great news, Lucy."

"What?"

"Jared Wetherly called me this morning. Right after I hung up with you."

Lucy stared at him. "Called you? From where?"

"I assume from the place he's staying. Although he sounded like he was in a cave or something—it had a funny echo."

Was there a phone in the church cellar? She didn't remember one.

"He's ready to meet his grandmother." Matt sounded pleased.

"He is?" Lucy told herself she shouldn't really be surprised. She'd seen how Jared's wound had miraculously healed. And he couldn't hide forever. Sooner or later he'd have to face what was left of his family and reconnect at some level. She knew she should feel glad about it, but for some strange reason it depressed her.

Matt helped her into the Jeep, then sat down

behind the wheel. "I'll drop you off at Mrs. Wetherly's. You and she can have a nice chat while I go pick up Jared—and then we'll all sit down to Mrs. Dempsey's pot roast and homemade apple pie."

"Sounds good," Lucy agreed without enthusiasm. "Where are you picking him up?"

"You know that bed-and-breakfast on the north edge of town?"

"You mean Stratton House?"

Matt looked dubious. "I . . . think that's it. All I know is that it backs right up to the woods."

The woods. Was that where Jared had been attacked, she wondered? But there were lots and lots of woods around here . . . it could have happened any place. *Like the woods behind Irene's house . . . like the woods around the park . . .*

"Are you okay?" Matt eased up on the accelerator and gave her an anxious glance.

"Sure."

"You seem a million miles away."

"Just thinking."

He slowed at a railroad crossing and glanced at her again. "It's gonna be fine, you know. She'll love you."

"Thanks. But that's not what I was thinking about."

Before he could respond, Lucy turned and fixed him with a solemn frown.

"Do you remember when Byron died, and you went to Gran's house to tell her?"

Matt looked puzzled. "Yes."

"You said the front door was unlocked, and she was sitting up in bed, just like she was waiting for you."

Matt nodded, but didn't speak.

"So here we are, not saying anything to her so she won't worry. But what if she already knows? What if she knew before we did?"

Matt considered this. They were on Gran's street now, and Lucy could see the Victorian house at the end of the cul-de-sac. The two of them sat there while the Jeep idled at the curb.

"How could she know about Jared?" Matt asked reasonably. "She *lived* with Byron—she *raised* Byron. They were close."

"How did she seem when you told her Jared was here?"

"I haven't told her yet."

"Matt!"

"I know, I know, but he asked me not to. He said he wanted to tell her himself, in private. He said he wanted it to be personal and . . . and special."

"You're the one who said another shock might kill her!"

"Well, I thought maybe if you were there with her, it wouldn't."

"You're the priest. You're the one who's supposed to be good at handling things like this."

"Who told you that?" But at Lucy's sigh of exasperation, Matt rushed on. "Look, all I'm saying is, there's no possible way she could know that Jared's coming here. There's no . . . connection like she had with Byron. She wouldn't necessarily have any memories of Jared if his father took him away that young. Maybe she wasn't even living here when it happened. Maybe she never even knew about Jared at all."

"How could she know about Byron and not Jared?" Lucy insisted. "How could she not—"

"I'm late," Matt broke in. "Sorry, but I've got to go across town . . ."

"That should take a good five minutes."

"Funny. I'll be back in a little while."

Lucy got out of the Jeep, but Matt added one last thing.

"Lucy—about that headstone. I think you're right about Irene. I don't want her to be there when I take it."

Lucy gave a distracted nod. She couldn't think about the headstone now—not with Jared and Gran to deal with. She could see Mrs. Dempsey waiting for her in the front doorway, yet she stood there on the curb, watching Matt drive away.

She didn't know why this was bothering her so much—this link between Jared and his grandmother. She supposed it was because Byron had told her about Gran's ability to "see" things before they happened. But maybe Matt was right. Maybe Gran never even knew about Jared. Maybe Jared had been a well-kept secret.

Lucy walked up the sidewalk to the porch. Mrs. Dempsey was glaring at her.

"She wants to see you right away. I got the house fixed up just the way she likes it. Special occasion and all."

"It looks beautiful," Lucy agreed, noting the

thoughtful touches Mrs. Dempsey had added. As on Lucy's previous visit, everything gleamed and shone; there wasn't a speck of dust to be found. Vases of fresh flowers filled the house with fragrance, wafting together with the comforting smell of roast beef and fresh-baked bread. The same large cat was here as well— only this time it watched Lucy from behind an umbrella stand in the hall.

Yes, Lucy thought suddenly, and with some surprise. *Yes, this is where I belong.*

It seemed so right somehow.

Almost as if she were coming home.

"Well, go on now." Mrs. Dempsey broke into Lucy's reverie. "She's waiting."

Lucy remembered her way to the bedroom. She walked down the hallway, then paused a moment right outside the door.

Gran motioned her in before Lucy even knocked.

Still lying in the old-fashioned bed, surrounded by fluffy white covers and soft stacked pillows trimmed in delicate lace. Her nightgown was still the color of cream, and her long braid of silvery hair still fell across one tiny, thin shoulder. It was obvious that she'd been beautiful when she was young. She still was.

"Big day," Lucy said, almost shyly. She walked toward the bed, then began to notice that Gran wasn't smiling. That those huge dark eyes, so much like Byron's, were pinned intently on Lucy's face.

Lucy faltered. "I . . . I don't know how to thank you, Mrs. Wetherly. Byron loved you so much. I just feel . . . honored."

Finally . . . a feeble attempt at a smile. Gran moved her left hand again and gestured Lucy to come closer.

"What is it?" Lucy asked softly. "Is there something you want me to do?"

She could see the slate and the piece of chalk.

The painstaking movement of Gran's palsied hand as it scratched childlike letters across the surface of the slate.

DANGER.

Lucy reached out in slow motion. Trembling, she closed her fingers around Gran's.

"What is it?" she murmured. "What's wrong?"

"We're here!" Matt called from the porch.

And Gran was looking at her with such emotion—such profound emotion in those midnight eyes—but Lucy couldn't read it, didn't know what Gran was trying to tell her. Unsure what else to do, she turned the slate over and tucked it beneath the covers, talking gently to Gran the whole time.

"Mrs. Dempsey is going to show me everything I need to learn—the way you like the house kept, and what you like to eat, and—"

Footsteps came striding down the hall.

"—your favorite books and flowers . . ."

Matt stepped across the threshold and gave Gran his warmest smile.

"Mrs. Wetherly," he said softly, "there's someone I'd like you to meet."

Jared was standing behind Matt, and now Lucy saw him come forward. She heard her own breath catching in her throat—she felt herself clutching Gran's shoulder.

"Grandmother?" Jared's voice quivered, and his eyes shone with tears. "I . . . after all this time . . . I don't know what to say."

Lucy didn't either.

For this wasn't the Jared she'd rescued.

The Jared she'd hidden in the church cellar . . . the one she'd tried to save . . .

This tall young man standing before her now was someone else.

Someone she'd never seen before in her life.

**TURN THE PAGE FOR A SNEAK PEEK AT
THE NEXT CHILLING INSTALLMENT**

Prologue

The Game, at last, was drawing to a close.

The Game he could well have played out indefinitely, stalking Lucy into final and desperate submission.

But now that his hand had been unexpectedly forced, he would stand and claim what was rightfully his.

Stand and *fight* for what was rightfully his.

Yes, it is best this way.

Even for a master of deceit such as himself, lies could grow tiresome after so long. Flowing and fluent lies, cloaked in tragedies. Sad and seductive lies, veiled in sorrows.

Lies that slipped so easily into Lucy's tender heart, begging pity and compassion.

Lies that brought her closer.

Lies that made her trust.

Your weaknesses are my strengths, Lucy.

And now he would be stronger than ever.

No matter that the attack in the cemetery had taken him completely by surprise. Or that the ensuing battle, though brief, had been savagely brutal.

Lucy was to blame for all of it.

Lucy, the cause of his inattention, the source of his carelessness.

A distraction he could no longer afford.

So now the Game must end.

He closed his eyes, wincing slightly, touching the bruised and bloodied skin along his side.

The last of his wounds had practically disappeared. The pain had faded off into one more bitter memory.

But the *old* wounds, the *ancient* wounds, had festered for hundreds of years, and the old scars still burned deep.

And though there had been many other battles in the past, none had ever been so important as the one he would soon be facing.

For his birthright . . .

His bloodline . . .

And for all eternity . . .

For you, my Lucy.

1

If only she'd known what was about to happen.

If only she'd been able to see how much worse, how much darker, the tragedies were that lay just ahead of her.

But it was Sunday, and she and Matt were going to Gran's, and for a few brief moments, she actually allowed herself a flicker of optimism.

So Lucy didn't know, and Lucy didn't see all those horrors yet to come.

And even if she had . . . it was already too late.

She'd been so excited when Matt picked her up that morning.

Excited about having dinner at Gran's house, but even more thrilled that Gran had invited her to live there while Irene was away in Paris.

And then Matt had given her the unexpected

news: "Jared Wetherly called me this morning. Right after I hung up with you."

"Called you? From where?"

"I assume from the place he's staying. Although he sounded like he was in a cave or something— it had a funny echo."

Her mind had instantly switched to Jared. He'd been asleep when she'd last checked on him. He'd been asleep in the hiding place, and she hadn't woken him up. And now Matt was saying that Jared had *called*? Was there a phone in the church cellar? She couldn't remember one.

"He's ready to meet his grandmother," Matt announced then.

He'd sounded so pleased about it. And though Lucy hadn't exactly anticipated this turn of events, she'd told herself she shouldn't *really* be surprised. She'd seen how Jared's wound had miraculously healed. And Jared couldn't hide forever. Sooner or later he'd have to face what was left of his family and reconnect at some level. In her heart, she'd known she should feel glad about it, but for some strange reason it had only depressed her.

4

"I'll drop you off at Mrs. Wetherly's," Matt told her. "You and she can have a nice chat while I go pick up Jared—and then we'll all sit down to Mrs. Dempsey's pot roast and homemade apple pie."

But Lucy hadn't felt much enthusiasm. "Where are you picking him up?"

"You know that bed-and-breakfast on the north edge of town?"

"You mean Stratton House?"

"I . . . think that's it. All I know is that it backs right up to the woods."

The woods. Was that where Jared had been attacked? she wondered. But there were lots and lots of woods around here . . . it could have happened any place. *Like the woods behind Irene's house . . . like the woods around the park . . .*

"Are you okay?" Easing up on the accelerator, Matt had given her an anxious glance.

"Sure."

"You seem a million miles away."

"Just thinking."

He slowed at a railroad crossing and glanced at her again. "It's gonna be fine, you know. She'll love you."

"Thanks. But that's not what I was thinking about."

Before he could respond, Lucy turned and fixed him with a solemn frown.

"Do you remember when Byron died, and you went to Gran's house to tell her?"

Matt looked puzzled. "Yes."

"You said the front door was unlocked, and she was sitting up in bed, just like she was waiting for you."

Matt nodded, but didn't speak.

"So here we are, not saying anything to her so she won't worry. But what if she already knows? What if she knew before we did?"

Matt had considered this. They'd turned onto Gran's street, and Lucy could see the Victorian house at the end of the cul-de-sac. The two of them sat there while the Jeep idled at the curb.

"How *could* she know about Jared?" Matt asked reasonably. "She *lived* with Byron—she *raised* Byron. They were close."

"How did she seem when you told her Jared was here?"

"I haven't told her yet."

"Matt!"

"I know, I know, but he asked me not to. He said he wanted to tell her himself. He said he wanted it to be personal and . . . and special."

"You're the one who said another shock might kill her!"

"Well, I thought maybe if you were there with her, it wouldn't."

"You're the priest. You're the one who's supposed to be so good at handling things like this."

"Who told you that?" But at Lucy's sigh of exasperation, Matt had rushed on. "Look, all I'm saying is, there's no possible way she could know that Jared's coming here. There's no . . . connection, like she had with Byron. She wouldn't necessarily have any memories of Jared, if his father took him away that young. Maybe she wasn't even living here when it happened. Maybe she never even knew about Jared at all."

"How could she know about Byron and not Jared?" Lucy insisted. "How could she not—"

"I'm late," Matt broke in. "Sorry, but I've got to go across town."

"That should take a good five minutes."

"Funny. I'll be back in a little while."

Lucy had gotten out of the Jeep, but Matt added one last thing.

"Lucy—about that headstone. I think you're right about Irene. I don't want her to be there when I take it."

Lucy had given a distracted nod. She couldn't think about the headstone now—not with Jared and Gran to deal with. She could see Mrs. Dempsey waiting for her in the front doorway, yet she stood there on the curb, watching Matt drive away.

She didn't know why this was bothering her so much—this link between Jared and his grandmother. She supposed it was because Byron had told her about Gran's ability to "see" things before they happened. But maybe Matt was right. Maybe Gran never even knew about Jared. Maybe Jared had been a well-kept secret.

She'd walked up the sidewalk to the porch. Mrs. Dempsey had been glaring at her.

"She wants to see you right away. I got the house fixed up, just the way she likes it. Special occasion and all."

"It looks beautiful," Lucy agreed, noting the thoughtful touches Mrs. Dempsey had added. As on Lucy's previous visit, everything gleamed and shone; there wasn't a speck of dust to be found. Vases of fresh flowers filled the house with fragrance, wafting together with the comforting smell of roast beef and fresh-baked bread. The same large cat was here as well—only this time it watched Lucy from behind an umbrella stand in the hall.

Yes, Lucy had thought suddenly, and with some surprise. *Yes, this is where I belong.*

It had seemed so right somehow.

Almost as if she were coming home.

"Well, go on now." Mrs. Dempsey broke into Lucy's reverie. "She's waiting."

Lucy remembered her way to the bedroom. She walked down the hallway, then paused a moment right outside the door.

Gran motioned her in before Lucy even knocked.

Still lying in the old-fashioned bed, surrounded by fluffy white covers and soft stacked pillows trimmed in delicate lace. Her nightgown was still the color of cream, and her long braid

9

of silvery hair still fell across one tiny, thin shoulder. It was obvious that she'd been beautiful when she was young. She still was.

"Big day," Lucy said, almost shyly. She walked toward the bed, then began to notice that Gran wasn't smiling. That those huge dark eyes, so much like Byron's, were pinned intently on Lucy's face.

Lucy faltered. "I . . . I don't know how to thank you, Mrs. Wetherly. Byron loved you so much. I just feel . . . honored."

Finally . . . a feeble attempt at a smile. Gran moved her left hand again and gestured for Lucy to come closer.

"What is it?" Lucy asked softly. "Is there something you want me to do?"

She could see the slate and the piece of chalk.

The painstaking movement of Gran's palsied hand as it scratched childlike letters across the surface of the slate.

DANGER.

Lucy reached out in slow motion. Trembling, she closed her fingers around Gran's.

"What is it?" she murmured. "What's wrong?"

"We're here!" Matt called from the porch.

And Gran had been looking at her with such emotion—such profound emotion in those midnight eyes—but Lucy couldn't read it, didn't know what Gran was trying to tell her. Unsure what else to do, she turned the slate over and tucked it beneath the covers, talking gently to Gran the whole time.

"Mrs. Dempsey is going to show me everything I need to learn: the way you like the house kept, and what you like to eat, and—"

Footsteps came striding down the hall.

"Your favorite books and flowers—"

Matt stepped across the threshold and gave Gran his warmest smile. "Mrs. Wetherly," he said softly, "there's someone I'd like you to meet."

Jared was standing behind Matt, but now Lucy saw him come forward. She heard her own breath catching in her throat . . . she felt herself clutching Gran's shoulder.

"Mrs. Wetherly?" Jared had sounded slightly uncomfortable. After one quick glance, he'd gazed at the floor. "I . . . after all this time . . . I don't know what to say."

Lucy hadn't known either.

For this wasn't the Jared she'd rescued.

The Jared she'd hidden in the church cellar . . . the one she'd tried to save . . .

This tall young man standing beside her now was someone else.

Someone she'd never seen before in her life.

2

"Lucy?"

Had someone spoken? Had someone said her name?

"Lucy, I want you to meet Jared."

Or was she just imagining it?

The voice seemed oddly familiar, yet, at the same time, distant and disconnected —the same way *she* was feeling disconnected from this silent tableau around her: Matt in the doorway with a puzzled frown; Mrs. Dempsey behind him in the hall, wiping her eyes with a balled-up handkerchief; Gran lying so small and still in the bed, with Lucy's hand still clutching her shoulder. And all of them staring at the young man who'd suddenly walked into their midst.

The young man Lucy had never seen before.

"Lucy?"

Who *was* that? Lucy was sure she knew the voice but was at a loss to identify it. She was sure she knew the room, and the house, but, for that same inexplicable reason, sensed that everything had suddenly changed.

Am I the only one who's noticed?

The faces around her certainly didn't seem concerned. Except for Matt, who appeared to be saying something and trying to make eye contact with her.

Something's *different*.

With concentrated effort, Lucy tried to pinpoint the answer. *Good something? Bad something?* But she couldn't decide; her thoughts told her nothing.

"Lucy!"

Matt's voice broke through at last, scattering those thoughts in all directions. Startled, Lucy saw his face come into sharp focus and realized that no one was watching the young man anymore; they were all looking at her.

"I'm . . ." She glanced around, flushing in embarrassment. "I'm sorry . . . what?"

"I said, this is Jared Wetherly. Jared, this is Lucy."

She realized then that she hadn't taken her gaze off Jared Wetherly since he'd first come through the door. That her perceptions of everyone and everything else had come from other senses, but that her sight and attention had been firmly fixed on this long-lost grandson who had so recently—and conveniently—shown up out of nowhere.

My God, he could be a prince.

This was the first impression that came to her, as her eyes drifted over his hair, his face, down the length of his body.

A prince with night-black eyes.

Those Wetherly eyes, so much like Byron's, deep and dark and fathomless, unsettlingly intense. Eyes that could hold an interminable stare; eyes unhindered by shadows.

Eyes that can see into souls . . .

Eyes that reminded her all too well of that other stranger, that other Jared she'd rescued and cared for, that other Jared who'd claimed to be Byron's brother . . .